The Sylvia Game

The Sylvia Game

Vivien Alcock

Houghton Mifflin Company
Boston   1997

For information about this and other Houghton Mifflin trade
and reference books and multimedia products, visit
The Bookstore at Houghton Mifflin on the World Wide Web
at http://www.hmco.com/trade/.

First published by Methuen Children's Books Ltd.,
London, England, 1982
Published by Mammoth, an imprint of Reed Consumer Books Limited,
London, England, 1992

First American edition

The text of this book is set in 12.5 point Simoncini Garamond.

Library of Congress Cataloging-in-Publication Data
Alcock, Vivien.
The Sylvia game / by Vivien Alcock.
p.   cm.
Summary:
During a trip to the seaside with her ne'er-do-well artist father,
twelve-year-old Emily makes friends with a gypsy's son and the
young heir to a stately home, who are struck by her resemblance
to mysterious, long-dead Sylvia, a girl in a painting by Renoir.

ISBN 0-395-81650-5
[1. Mystery and detective stories.   2. Fathers and
daughters—Fiction.   3. Artists—Fiction.   4. Painting—Fiction.]
I. Title.
PZ7.A334Sy   1997
[Fic] — dc21   96-53109   CIP   AC

Printed in the United States of America
MV   10   9   8   7   6   5   4   3   2   1

To Iris

1

In October, Emily Dodd had the flu so badly that she nearly died of it. Everybody said so. For ten days she tossed and turned from one tangled nightmare to another, trying to escape from two men in raincoats who she knew must never catch her, though she could not remember why.

"Don't let them in!" she moaned. "Don't open the door!"

"Hush! It's all right, my pet," her father said softly. "Lie still. Don't move, little Emily."

As she shut her eyes, she seemed to hear the soft whisper of charcoal on paper. He was drawing her again, but she was too ill to care. She was glad, in her brief waking moments, to see him always there on the chair by her bed, his small bright eyes intent upon her face.

It was her mother who minded. When Emily awoke, cool at last but so weak that she could hardly keep her eyes open against the gray light of a wet afternoon, she heard her mother say in a low voice, "I don't know how you can! Honestly, Ben, I don't! When she's been so ill — somehow it doesn't seem right."

"Why ever not?" asked her father, surprised.

Emily turned her head on the pillow. She was lying on a bed in the corner of her father's studio, her own room having been thought too small and dark and damp for an invalid, as indeed were most of the rooms in their semi-basement flat, except for this one, with its tall windows onto the garden and its good north light. The screen that had been round her bed (it was the one behind which the models had undressed in the days when her father could afford a model) had been folded back. She could see her father and mother standing looking at a canvas on the easel. Her mother was still in her raincoat and headscarf, and had obviously just come back from work. She looked tired.

"I don't know," she was saying. "It just seems — sort of heartless to me. Anyway, who'd want to buy it? A sick child — it's hardly cheerful, is it?"

Mr. Dodd sighed heavily. Emily knew what that

2

sigh meant. It meant he was an artist and had a mind above money — unlike his wife and his daughter and his small son, who complained because they couldn't have a new telly, or proper holidays or new clothes.

"One has to be true to something in this life," he would tell them, beaming virtuously. "Whatever my faults — and I'd be the first to admit that I have a few — at least I'm true to my talent. To my art."

And Emily and Tim would scowl, for they didn't care a button for his art, but only wished he'd get a proper job, so their mother wouldn't have to go to work at the factory, coming home tired with all the cooking and washing and ironing yet to be done while their father just sat on a chair and drew her doing it. *Portrait of a Woman Peeling Potatoes. Study of a Woman Darning Socks.* Painting after painting that nobody wanted to buy.

So now when her mother said she would get their tea, Emily felt well enough to say angrily, "Mum's tired. *She's* been working. You get the tea, Dad."

"That sounds more like our Emily," said her father, coming over to her bed. "You're on the road to recovery, darling."

3

A long, dismal road. Now Emily would no longer let her father draw her but turned her head away fretfully, pulling the sheet right over her face while she wept behind it. She cried all the time. When her brother was at school, she cried because she was lonely. When he came home, she cried because he was noisy, knocked over her jigsaw, and scribbled all over her books.

"Emily's bloody wet," said Tim.

"Don't swear," she snapped, "or I'll tell Mum."

"This isn't like my little Emily," said her father.

"I'm not your *little* Emily," she said furiously. "I'm twelve!"

"Ah, but you're small for your age," he said, with what he obviously thought was a winning smile. He wouldn't get any prizes from her! People often told her how charming her father was. She didn't find him so. Not any longer! Once she had been happy just to be with him, washing his brushes, cleaning his palette, posing for him until she itched all over with suppressed fidgets. She had not minded that they were often poor, when they seemed at other times so rich. Whenever Mr. Dodd sold a painting, he would come home laden with champagne, smoked salmon, grapes, and silly, pretty presents for her and Tim.

"Oh, *Ben!*" her mother would say. "I do wish you wouldn't! What about the rent? And that electricity bill?"

But her father would just laugh and say that life would be too dull without a little celebration now and then.

"Don't worry," he'd say. "I'm rich today. Just leave the bills to me."

And when the electricity was cut off, so that they had to have cold tomato soup by candlelight, he would tell them ghost stories, and try to make their mother laugh, and promise he would pay the bill the very next day.

Then one day the bailiffs came and took their furniture away, leaving only their beds, stranded on a desert of bare boards, their mother's saucepans, and the tools of their father's trade (which, he claimed, meant everything in his studio, down to the paint-spattered rug on the floor). "Ah well," he'd said cheerfully, surveying their ravaged home. "Now we have room for improvement." And suddenly Emily, seeing her mother cry, looked at her father with new eyes. He was a fool! A fat, idle, extravagant fool!

She still loved him, she supposed — she could not help it. But not in the same way! Now when

5

he bought her presents, she would look at them coldly, and ask, "How much did that cost?"

"Oh, *Emily!* It's pretty! You'll look lovely in it."

A shawl with pink roses and a fringe a foot long. A stupid white dress, all frills and tucks and green ribbons —

"I won't wear it! I hate it! Everybody'd laugh! You only bought it because you want me to pose in it. Well, I won't!"

But she had, of course. An unpaid model, that's all she was to him. He was the most selfish person in the world.

"What a cross little face," he was saying now. "What about a smile for your dear old dad?"

"Leave me alone!" she screamed.

"Oh, my God!" said her father, losing his patience. "It's high time you were back at school."

The doctor would not hear of it. She was suffering from post-influenzal depression, he said next morning, and needed building up. A change of air, perhaps.

"You haven't got an aunt who lives at the seaside, have you?" he asked, smiling at her.

"No."

"Pity."

"I'll have to see what I can do," said her father. "I'm sure I can manage something. No trouble." A look of almost guilty amusement came into his face, as if he had suddenly decided to give way to some temptation. "Dorset . . . How would you like ten days by the sea, Emily? In a hotel? Just you and me?"

Emily looked at him stonily. Did he imagine she was going to *thank* him? Did he think he was impressing *her?* What had happened to the week in Weymouth last year? Not to mention the cottage in Devon the year before? A day trip to Southend was all they'd ever got! Promises! Promises cost nothing!

"Where's the money going to come from?" asked her mother, when she heard about it.

"Don't you worry your pretty little heads about that. Just leave it to me," he said.

Emily saw her mother look at him sharply, suspiciously, and she held her breath.

"Have you sold a painting, Ben?"

"I do sell paintings occasionally. I know my family has no respect for me, but . . ."

"*Which* painting?"

"Well, I haven't actually sold it yet, but things

7

are moving in the right direction, you might say. And I've a little business on hand . . ."

"*What* business?"

"Oh, a little bit of this and that," said Mr. Dodd evasively. He hated to commit himself. "A little bit of this and that."

Mrs. Dodd opened her mouth as if she would have liked to question him further, but shut it again when she saw her daughter, all ears.

"I don't want to go!" said Emily quickly, hoping to take the worried look off her mother's face.

But her mother said they would have to see. All evening she kept glancing at Mr. Dodd with a sharp, questioning look. Emily wondered uneasily what her mother suspected. It wasn't the bills — they'd all been paid last week. There was something else . . .

Her father had been behaving strangely for months. Had taken to locking the studio door at times, refusing to let anybody in. Had gone away for odd nights, offering excuses her mother obviously found difficult to accept. His very face, once so open and guileless, now often wore a look of secret, shifty pleasure, like a child with a hidden bag of sweets he'd no intention of sharing.

Her father was up to something. Emily wished she knew what.

Five days later, Tim was watching her pack.

"Lucky pig!" he said. "It's not fair! Why can't I come too?"

"You haven't had the flu."

"Mum given you any spending money?"

She nodded.

"How much?"

"Never you mind."

"Give us a bit," he said hopefully, holding out his hand and smiling his most engaging little-boy smile. He looked just like their father, she thought.

"No."

"Come on, just a little. Fifty pence?"

"No."

"Ten pence?"

"No."

"You never give me anything nowadays!" he complained. "You're a lousy old miser!"

She nodded. "I want to be very rich," she explained, "and you have to start young."

"I'm going to be very rich, too," he said.

"No, you're not. You're too like Dad. You

9

spend all your money as soon as you get it. Now me, I'm going to have a large house with servants and cars and a color telly. You can come and stay if you like."

"Don't want to! I'll be a terrorist and come and blow up your house with a bomb."

"I'll just buy another."

"No, you won't! You'll be dead! Dead! Dead! Dead!" he cried, bouncing up and down on her bed and making the springs squeak. Then his face changed and he flung himself on her, in tears.

"I didn't mean it! Don't die, Emily! Don't die!"

"Stupid!" she said, laughing. "I'm not going to! You can't make things happen just by saying them, you clot."

"You can, then! Dad said so!"

"*Dad!*" she said scornfully. "Then why doesn't he say he's a great painter whose pictures are worth millions? You disgusting brat, your nose is running all over the place. Look, here's a hanky. Damn, it's a paint rag. Now you've got a blue nose! It rather suits you," she said, trying to cheer him up, for he looked so small and woebegone. "I think, just for your blue nose, I might give you fifty p after all."

When it was safely in his hand, he ran out of the room, laughing.

"You'll never be rich now!" he said.

Next morning, her mother hugged her and kissed her, saying, "You will be careful, Emily? Don't go out without wrapping up well. Keep your anorak zipped up. Wear a scarf. Put your hood up if it rains. Change your socks the minute you get back to the hotel if you get your feet wet —"

"*Mum!* Don't fuss."

Her mother looked at her and it seemed to Emily there was another, deeper anxiety in her eyes.

"Mum, are you sure we can afford it?" she asked.

But her mother merely said, "Oh, Emily. Don't always think about money. I don't know what's come over you lately. You never used to be like this. Don't be such a little worrier. I want you to enjoy yourself."

"Haven't you got one old flu germ left for me?" said Tim, flinging himself upon her.

As she fended him off, laughing, she saw her mother's face, abstracted, uneasy, and said impulsively, "Don't worry about Dad. I'll look after him. I won't let him . . ."

"Won't let him what?" said her mother.

"Won't let him . . . See he doesn't . . . you know!"

"No, I don't know, Emily. What are you talking about?"

"I just mean — I — I don't know," said Emily, wishing she'd never started. She could not put her suspicions into words. Not even to herself.

Her mother looked as if she would have liked to have said more, but Tim went whooping down the path, saying he would be late for school, and she had to follow him.

"Well, Emily," her father said, "are you convinced at last we're really going? Oh!" He rubbed his hands together. "You and I are going to have a splendid time."

"Yes," she said, smiling up at him, determined not to suspect him of anything.

But down at the bottom of her mind, a voice kept saying, Where did he get the money for this holiday? Where did he get the money?

2

The Fairview Hotel did not live up to its name. It was on a side street and faced onto a terrace of similar small hotels and guest houses, all wearing striped blinds like medal ribbons from past summers.

The place was nearly empty. The food, Emily thought, had probably finished off the weaker visitors. Meat was covered with a thick brown sauce, and fish with a thick white sauce, and chicken, she suspected, by a combination of the two.

"Let's eat out tomorrow," her father said.

"But we're paying for this, aren't we?" said Emily. "Whether we eat it or not, I mean?"

"Oh, Emily!" he sighed. "Don't always think about money. You're turning into a real little miser, aren't you?"

Weak tears filled her eyes but she was determined not to cry. In two days they had already done the town. They had eaten cream doughnuts in Mary's Parlor and éclairs in the Wishing Well. They had played the machines in the amusement arcade, sent postcards to Mum and Tim, and seen *Dinner with Dracula* at the only cinema.

This afternoon they had walked along the windy seafront, beneath a cold gray sky and beside a cold gray sea. Most of the small shops were already boarded up for the winter, their bright beachballs and buckets and spades put away. It gave the place a desolate air, which the seagulls' melancholy complaints did nothing to dispel. They were glad to return to the hotel.

"What about another game of checkers?" said Mr. Dodd, rubbing his hands together and trying to look delighted at the prospect. "Or snakes and ladders?"

He was already bored, thought Emily. She saw him glance wistfully toward the small, brightly lit hotel bar, which had just opened for the evening and where she was not allowed to sit.

"Go and have a drink, if you like, Dad. I'll be all right."

14

"No, no! I'm having fun here," he said untruthfully, beginning to lay out the black and white pieces. He glanced across the lounge to the only other occupants, a pair of old ladies, fast asleep in their chairs, and said, for perhaps the sixth time, "Pity there's no one young for you here. It's term time, of course — they're all back at school."

"It's all right. I like being with you."

He patted her hand, but did not say that he liked being with her. Instead he said casually, "Oh, by the way, I wondered if you'd mind amusing yourself tomorrow afternoon. I've something to attend to . . ."

"What? Where are you going?"

"Oh well, I've got things to do . . ." He waved his hand vaguely as if indicating a crowd of excuses from which she could take her pick.

"*What* things?"

"Really, Emily, you sound just like your mother! I — um — have to see a man in — in Bournemouth."

"I'll come with you! Why can't I? Take me with you! I want to go to Bournemouth."

"It's not exactly *in* Bournemouth," said her father, shifting his ground immediately, and awaking all Emily's suspicions. "It's just outside. Business.

15

There'd be nothing for you to do, Emmie. You'd be bored."

"I wouldn't! I'm bored here! I'm going to come!"

"No. I'm sorry, Emily," he said firmly.

She glared at him. Had he forgotten already she was an invalid, and had to be taken care of? Hadn't the doctor told him she was suffering from post-influenzal depression? Emily felt instinctively that this would cover a lot of bad behavior.

"You can't leave me! Supposing I drown myself?" she said.

"Oh, *Emily!*"

At that moment a boy came in with a basket of logs, which he set down beside the fire.

"Ah, what have we here?" said Mr. Dodd, turning to him with relief. "Do I really see someone under a hundred years old?"

"Dad!" said Emily, embarrassed.

The boy looked round, glanced briefly at Emily, and then back at her father.

"Sorry, mister. Was you talking to me?"

"Just saying how nice it is to see a young face. My poor daughter's bored with us old fogeys, aren't you, Emily? What's your name, lad? Kevin? Look,

I've an idea. You finish this game for me, Kevin, and I'll buy you both a Coke. How's that?"

He was gone before either of them could reply.

Emily's face burned. I hate him! she thought. How could he do this to me?

She looked at the boy and saw he was staring at her, his dark eyes unenthusiastic. He was about her own age, with a broad, brown gypsy face and black hair curling to his shoulders. In one ear he wore a gold ring.

"I got work to do," he said.

"Don't let me stop you," she said coldly.

"Sorry, miss."

"Don't be. It wasn't my idea."

He shrugged and, turning to the fire, began poking it.

Emily stared resentfully at the door to the bar. Her father, no doubt, would take his time coming back with the Cokes, hoping that she and the boy would become acquainted in his absence. Probably hoping she would suddenly acquire a host of friends in Swanham Bay so that he could go off on his own unhindered.

Go where? What was he up to now? Whatever it was, she wouldn't let him get away with it. She'd promised her mother she'd look after him and she would, even if she had to . . . what? Follow him? Find out where he went?

Easier said than done, she suspected. Supposing he looked round? Right little fool she'd look, spying on her own father — not that he wasn't asking for it! She brooded, playing idly with the checkers on the board.

"You want to get rid of his pieces, silly, not your own. Look, that 'un's nearly a king — you can be ditching that for a start."

It was the boy. He had stopped fixing the fire and was kneeling on the floor, watching what she was doing.

"Are you suggesting I should cheat?"

"Wasn't that what you was at?"

"No."

"That be all right, then."

"I thought you had work to do."

"I thought I heard summat about a Coke."

"Did you? I don't remember."

He laughed. "You're a proper little liar! How old would you be? Ten?"

"Twelve," said Emily crossly, "and if you say I'm small for my age, *you'll* be smaller — by a head! So just watch it!"

"That be fighting talk, Titch! Who'll knock it off? *You?*" But he was smiling and his face for the first time looked friendly. He stood up. "I'm thirteen," he said. "Well? Ben't you going to say it?"

"Say what?"

"That I ben't a giant myself, exactly."

Emily, looking at him, saw for the first time that, though sturdy, he was not much taller than she was. It gave her an idea.

She said absently, "Aren't you? I hadn't noticed. You look all right to me." The boy looked pleased, but when she added, "You wouldn't do me a favor, would you?" his expression immediately changed to one of weary disillusion, as if he was used to people only being nice to him when they wanted something.

"A favor? I might've knowed," he said. "Well, perhaps. Depends what it is. And it will cost you."

"You mean — I'll have to pay?" she asked, shocked.

"A' course, Titch. What d'you expect? We're not old buddies, are we? What was it you wanted, then?"

She hesitated, on the brink of giving up the whole idea, when her father appeared, carrying two glasses of Coke. His face, when he saw the

19

boy was still there, lit up with such an expression of relief that Emily could have hit him. Had two days in her company really been so unbearable? Didn't it occur to him that she'd been bored silly by *him?*

"Having a nice game?" he said happily. "Good, good! Here are some potato chips, cheese and onion, isn't that what you like? Don't let me interrupt you. I'll be in the bar if you want me for anything."

And he was gone again. Emily, humiliated, looked at the boy.

"Don't fret, Titch. They're all alike," he said. "Let's get down to business. What d'you want?"

Now Emily had no hesitations at all.

"I want to borrow an old anorak or coat — only it mustn't be navy blue, because mine is. Just for tomorrow, you can have it back in the evening. And an old school scarf . . ."

His dark eyes were sharp with curiosity.

"What be you up to, Titch?"

"Mind your own business. I don't have to tell you. As you said, it's not as if we're old buddies, is it?"

"Fair enough. O.K. Now for my terms. One pound —"

"What!" Emily's shriek of horror awoke the two old ladies at the other side of the lounge. They sat up, blinking.

Kevin lowered his voice. "One pound down and fifty p back when you return the things."

"Don't you trust me?" she asked indignantly.

His mother, he informed her, was manageress of the Fairview Hotel, and the tales she could tell about disappearing towels and ashtrays and dud checks, you'd think the world was made up of thieves. Emily, opening her mouth to protest, thought of her father, hesitated, and blushed.

"All right," she said recklessly, though it hurt to think of parting with so much money.

He smiled. "You give up too easy. I'd have settled for half that," he said. "You won't never be rich." He sounded like Tim.

"I *will,*" she muttered fiercely, and he looked at her curiously.

"What for?" he asked.

"What?"

"What d'you want a lot of money for?"

To be safe, she thought. So that nobody could come knocking at her door, turning off the electricity, taking away the furniture . . . Two men in raincoats, looking at her with pity, and offering her a toffee, saying, "Sorry, love. We're just doing our job. Don't worry. You'll be all right. It's not the end of the world."

But all she said aloud was, "I don't know. Just because."

3

Mr. Dodd came jauntily out of the Fairview Hotel. A keen observer could not fail to notice (and resent) the holiday air about him, like a schoolboy let unexpectedly out of school. He ran lightly down the steps and went off along the street.

On the other side of the road, the keen observer, at last appearing satisfied with the shoelace it had been tying and retying for the past fifteen minutes, got to its feet. It was a small figure, wearing blue jeans, a jacket resembling that of a sergeant in the U.S. Army, a gray knitted balaclava hat, and racing goggles. It walked slowly in the same direction.

Now a third figure came out of a side entrance to the hotel, paused for a moment, and then sauntered casually in the rear.

The three figures turned the corner, one after another. None of them looked behind.

Five minutes later, Mr. Dodd paused at a bus stop, read the printed notice attached to it, nodded his head, and settled down to wait.

Emily, stopping to stare intently at some fishing rods in a convenient shop window, felt uncommonly foolish. She knew she must look silly and felt everyone was staring at her. The balaclava was hot and itchy, and her goggles kept steaming up so that she had to rub them with her fingers to make sure that it was her father she was following and not a complete stranger. Also, her nose and mouth, the only parts of her still visible, felt horribly exposed. One glance and he would surely say, "I know that nose. I've painted it! Oh, *Emily!*"

It had been a stupid idea. She had just decided to give up and return to the hotel when her hand was grasped, and a boy in a red woolen cap and sunglasses said in a hissing whisper, "Come on!"

Dragging her round the corner, he set off down the pavement at high speed, pulling her behind him. Furiously, she tried to free her hand.

"Let go! What are you doing! Let go!"

Tightening his grip, he said, "Come on or we'll

be too late!" and ran even faster, till she was too out of breath to protest.

At last he stopped abruptly and she saw they were at a request stop. There was no bus in sight.

"Guess who I am?" he said.

"Your earring's showing," she said coldly. She had recognized Kevin immediately.

"Real gold. Eighteen carat."

She said angrily, "You've been spying on me!" and then blushed.

"You're a fine one to talk," he said.

"Why aren't you at school?"

"It's my lunchtime. Mum said your dad had ordered an early lunch, so —"

"So you thought you'd come back and poke your nose in where it wasn't wanted!"

He looked offended. "I was only being friendly. Trying to help. Look what I brought you." He held out a comic book. "I punched a spyhole in it, so you can watch him through it. You'll be wanting to know when he gets off."

She did not know what to say. She took the comic book and looked at him helplessly, unable to offer any explanation for what she was doing.

"Say thank you, then, Titch. Your dad got a temper?"

"Yes."

"Best be careful, hadn't you? Here's the bus."

He put out his arm and the bus slowed to a stop. It was a single decker and had WAREHAM on the front.

"Supposing he doesn't get on?" she asked.

"There ben't another bus for over an hour. Must be this one."

On one side of the road, there was a large, bedraggled field, in which some black-and-white cows were sitting down. On the other side was a high wall, broken only by a driveway between two tall pillars. On each of these sat a stone animal, of doubtful pedigree but unmistakable ill nature.

The bus stopped.

"Mallerton House!" called the driver.

Mr. Dodd got off, and stood gazing round him with an enjoyment that nothing in the scenery seemed to justify.

The bus started up again. When it was round the next corner, the driver became aware of a child at his elbow, looking at him through a pair of enormous goggles which, with the gray balaclava it was wearing, made it look like a strange sort of insect.

"Please, was that Mallerton House? I'm supposed to get off there! I'll get lost!" and then, for good measure, although the driver, muttering something about the washing out of ears, was already slowing down, "I feel sick! Please let me off! I'm going to be sick!"

Emily thought she had managed that rather well. It was only when the bus was out of sight that her pleasure faded. It was a gray afternoon. The sun was hidden and there was a cold wind. She walked slowly back down the road until she came to the entrance to the house.

The tall, rusty iron gates stood open. She saw a pale, narrow drive winding out of sight between dark bushes and tall trees. There was no sign of her father. On one of the gateposts was a faded wooden board, saying:

MALLERTON HOUSE
Open to the public Monday to Friday 2–6 P.M.
House £1
Grounds only 50p. Maze 10p.
Children half-price.

A stately home, of all places! Was he planning to fill his pockets with family silver — under the watchful eye of the guide? I must've been mad, she thought. Thank God I didn't tell Mum what I suspected. Dad a thief! How could I have been so stupid?

He'd just lied to avoid any fuss. He'd known she wouldn't agree to come. Too many dull Sundays, she and Tim had fidgeted beside him, while a guide's voice droned like a bluebottle. Penned in by red ropes like cattle, warned off by notices — DO NOT TOUCH. PRIVATE. KEEP OUT. QUEUE HERE FOR THE TOILETS. QUEUE HERE FOR THE CAFETERIA . . .

One day, she thought, I'll have a house like this, and it'll be me behind the red ropes, sitting on the brocaded chair, eating off a gold plate. But now . . .

She could hardly follow her father into the house undetected. She looked again at the notice. The grounds? Even half-price was expensive.

A voice said sharply, "Yes?" in so forbidding a tone that it sounded more like no.

Emily looked round, startled, and noticed for the first time that there was a lodge on the right side of the drive, disguised with ivy into the likeness of a square shrub. One of the windows had a sign above it, saying TICKETS. PLEASE RING. An old woman, with a face so lined it looked as if someone had tried to scribble it out, stood behind a counter, watching her.

"Did you want anything?" she asked.

"Can you tell me the time of the next bus back to Swanham Bay, please?"

The woman clicked her tongue against her teeth disapprovingly, as much as to say she was not there to answer questions but to sell tickets. However, she told Emily she had just missed one. There wouldn't be another now till five o'clock.

Two hours! Emily looked again at the board.

"Are there any animals?" she asked.

"Animals? What sort of animals were you thinking of?"

"Oh, lions and giraffes and baboons," said Emily hopefully. Surely they must have something to offer for her twenty-five pence.

"We're not a safari park," said the woman, unsmiling. "We just have the house. And there's nothing there that would interest *you*," she added, looking Emily up and down disparagingly. "And the grounds aren't at their best at this time of year."

Emily began to have the feeling she was not welcome.

"I'll have a ticket to the Maze, please," she said.

"Five pence for the Maze and twenty-five for the grounds —"

"No. Just the Maze, please."

"You can't get to the Maze without going through the grounds, now can you?" the woman pointed out. "Thirty pence, please."

Emily fingered the money in her pocket. She tried an ingratiating smile. "Supposing I promise not to look at the grounds?" she said, but the woman shook her head. She doesn't like me, thought Emily, and then remembered her odd appearance. Taking off the balaclava and goggles, she shook out her hair.

The woman stared.

"Oh!" she said, strangely startled by this transformation of a hooded urchin into a pale girl with bright hair. "*Who are you!* Who are you, miss?"

"Why — my name is Emily. Emily Dodd."

"Dodd," repeated the woman slowly, and shook her head. "Sorry. You — reminded me of someone. Just for a moment. Are you from these parts?"

"No. From London. We're just staying in Swanham Bay."

"Funny," said the woman, still staring at her.

"Mum said her granny came from Corfe," Emily offered, "but that was ages ago. Before I was born."

"Ah, that would be it," said the woman, and as Emily looked surprised, added, "You have a — Dorset face, miss," and gave a little smile, too small for Emily to share.

"Can't I just have a ticket to the Maze, then?" asked Emily.

"Well . . . seeing you have a Dorset face, miss, perhaps we can make an exception." The woman took up a roll of blue tickets, but stood with it in her hand, still staring at Emily. Emily fidgeted under her gaze, beginning to feel uncomfortable. "Well, here you are, miss. One ticket to the Maze," she said finally. "Don't get lost now! Don't get lost!"

"I won't," said Emily.

"Children have got lost before now," said the woman warningly, and then added something half under her breath. Emily turned round in surprise, but the woman had already gone from the window. Could she really have said, "This is an unlucky house for children like you"?

4

It had rained earlier. Water shone at the bottom of the deep potholes in the drive and freckled the dark foliage of the evergreens. Emily tried to catch the yellow leaves that blew down about her as she walked. Someone had told her it was lucky to catch one, but always at the last moment the wind snatched them out of reach.

She needed luck. Her father must not see her like this, with her hair (pale cadmium orange, a very expensive color, he'd often complained) blowing out like a flag. Yet she could not bear to put on again the stifling balaclava. She walked slowly and silently.

Then, turning a corner, she found herself in the open, on the edge of a large garden of lawns and fountains and small hedges hardly high enough to hide a cat. On the far side lay a house, a low sprawling building of faded red brick and gray stone, whose tall chimneys, like clothespins, seemed to be holding it up to dry. It had a great many small windows, behind any one of which her father might be standing, gazing idly out.

The drive circled to the right and now she walked quickly, her feet loud on the gravel. She was glad when she came to a signpost whose one arm pointed down a grass path: TO THE MAZE. Here fir trees and shrubs hid her from the house and she walked more easily, until she saw ahead of her the tall, clipped hedges of the Maze.

There was a wrought-iron gate across the entrance, fastened with a padlock, and a notice, tied on the string, said CLOSED.

"I've paid!" she said indignantly, looking round for someone to complain to. But the only other living creature in this sad October garden was a shabby brown sparrow on the path.

She turned the cardboard notice over and saw, as she'd expected, that it said OPEN on the other side. Leaving it like this, written proof of her innocence, she climbed the gate and walked into the Maze.

It was very different from what she had imagined. The paths were of concrete, not grass, and littered everywhere with old cigarette packets and butts, candy wrappers, and lollipop sticks. The hedges, in spite of the rain, had a dusty, threadbare look. In places, large gaps near the ground were roughly filled in with wire netting.

"Five p for this!" grumbled Emily.

Yet somehow as she walked, following paths at random, the place began to charm her. It was so enclosed. Safe. No sound of traffic, no noise of people, no dogs barked in the distance, and no birds sang. There was only the soft sound of her feet on the path and a gentle sighing of a wind she could not feel. At any moment she might turn a corner and reach the heart of the Maze; or she might not. It was a place of endless alternatives.

The sun came out from the clouds. It turned the wire netting in the hedges into a silver embroidery and scattered golden coins on the shadowed paths. She was suddenly very happy. She thought of her father and the way he always walked, looking around with an air of pleased expectancy, as if he thought he would find something marvelous round the next corner, or the next — or in a hundred corners' time.

Now the sun went in again — and in the

sudden gloom there came the sound of weeping. Dismal, wretched, desolate, it disturbed the quiet air with its misery. Close at hand, behind this hedge or the next, someone was crying out a hopeless grief.

"It's all right!" Emily called, thinking it was a child lost. "I'm here! I'm coming!"

Immediately the weeping stopped, as if a hand had been clapped abruptly over a mouth.

She ran quickly up a path that seemed to lead the right way. But now the Maze turned malignant, as if the pitiful crying had aroused a streak of cruelty in its heart. The paths twisted and turned, seemed to promise — only to end in high, blank, forbidding hedges. Not this way. Nor this way. Try again. Backward and forward she ran until she was quite lost.

She stopped and listened. Her own ragged breathing sounded like sobs. She could hear no other.

"Where are you?" she called.

There was no answer.

"Are you there?"

Silence.

She was about to turn away when she heard, from behind the hedge on her right, a sort of muffled gulp. She looked up: the hedge was too high to climb, the thin twigs would not bear her weight. Then the sun came out again. Something glittered near her feet. It was a piece of wire netting covering a gap in the hedge.

She tore it out and flung it on the path. Then, getting down on hands and knees, she forced her way through the gap. Twigs and leaves flicked her face but she shut her eyes and pushed with her head — until it came out on the other side.

She found herself looking across a small lawn, brilliantly green in the stormy sunlight. On the far side stood a tall, thin, white-faced boy. His mouth hung open and his wild, light eyes stared down at her in terror. He looked mad, she thought uneasily, or at best only half-witted.

"Sylvia?" he said in a thin, high-pitched voice. "Sylvia?"

"No, it's me," said Emily soothingly, and pushing herself right through the hedge, she scrambled to her feet.

He looked her up and down, the fear in his eyes changing first to bewilderment, then to anger.

"Who are you? What do you want? What the devil are you doing here?" he asked furiously. She knew why he was so angry — it was because he had been caught crying like a baby, a boy of his age! She looked tactfully away from the tearstains on his cheeks.

"I was just walking in the Maze," she said innocently. "Is this the center?"

"No, of course not! This is the Lady Garden and it's private! Do you usually break your way through hedges? Is this how you treat other people's property?"

Her own temper rose.

"Look, I was just walking along, minding my own business, when I heard you . . ." She'd been going to say blubbering, but the sight of his white face softened her. He looked so ill. ". . . choking," she went on with scarcely a pause. "It's very dangerous to choke. You can die of it. A girl at my school choked on a ham sandwich last year and went blue in the face. Only then Mr. Banks, he's the math teacher, held her upside down and hit her, and it came out. The bit of ham, I mean."

"Really?" he said.

"Truly."

They looked at each other, both knowing she had made it up. The boy raised a hand and slowly brushed his wet cheeks, leaving dirty smudges. For a moment she thought he was going to reject the excuse she'd offered. But suddenly he smiled and said, "Beastly when something goes down the wrong way, isn't it?" He glanced at the hole in the hedge, but if he were thinking it was also beastly when something came out the wrong way, he did not say so. It was a truce.

Encouraged, she smiled back and asked the question that was intriguing her.

"Whom do I look like? I mean, whom did you take me for?" and, as he did not reply, she went on, "Who is Sylvia?"

He was silent for so long she thought he was not going to answer. An odd expression came into his face. He turned away as if to hide it, then, looking back over his shoulder, said, "My sister. But she's dead."

5

Dead! He'd taken her for a ghost! No wonder he'd looked terrified. She remembered the old woman in the lodge saying, "This is an unlucky house for children like you."

"I'm sorry," she said.

"It was a long time ago," he said, shrugging. "No one thinks of it now."

He was still staring at her. There were dark circles under his eyes and his face had a greenish pallor. Definitely he did not look healthy. Perhaps the whole family was affected by some horrible wasting disease; she wondered if it was catching, and edged away a little.

"Am I very like her?" she asked.

"Yes . . . perhaps," he said vaguely. "The color of your hair . . . and seeing your face like that, coming out of the leaves. It's how I always see her when I dream. I feel as if I'm dreaming now."

He was making her feel uneasy. As if she were not herself any longer but someone else.

"You're not dreaming," she said firmly.

"No," he agreed. "She'd never have worn such a silly jacket. I never thought of that."

"What's wrong with it?" asked Emily indignantly. "Anyway, it's not mine. I borrowed it. Don't keep staring at me as if I were a ghost. What happened to your sister? Was she ill?"

"She drowned. She got caught in the weeds and couldn't get free."

"Drowned!"

"Yes. In our lake. Would you like to see it?"

He said it quite cheerfully, as he might have offered to show her the banqueting hall or the bed where Queen Elizabeth had slept. Perhaps he always took visitors to see it, the lake where his sister had drowned. Morbid, Emily's mother would say disapprovingly. Whenever there was something unpleasant on television, she'd tell Emily not to look. "Shut your eyes," she'd say. "You don't want to look at that," and Emily would feel guilty, because of course she did.

The boy, not waiting for an answer, had walked

on. She followed him down a narrow path between high hedges into a deserted rose garden, the roses already pruned back into ugly thorny stumps. There were weeds growing between them, and a spade stuck into the earth looked rusty, as if it had been left out in the rain.

Emily, inspecting the boy surreptitiously as they walked, noticed that his coat looked shabby and too small for him, so that his thin wrists stuck out of the sleeves. There was a darn in his gray trousers.

She said, "Does your dad work here?"

"I'm Oliver Mallerton," he said, looking surprised, as if he thought everyone should know.

Oliver Mallerton of Mallerton House. How grand it sounded. Perhaps his father was a lord, or a duke, even. She supposed if you owned a great house like this, you didn't have to bother how you looked. You could let weeds grow in the rose beds and moths feed on your clothes and you'd still be Oliver Mallerton of Mallerton House. Lucky devil! What did he have to cry about? He had everything.

"What's your name?" he asked.

"Emily Dodd of Dodd Flat," she said. There was no doubt it didn't have quite the same ring to it.

He looked blank. "Where's that?"

"London."

"Oh, London!" he said, losing interest.

They walked on in silence. She noticed he kept turning to look at her, although when she caught his eye, he'd glance away immediately and start kicking idly at a stone on the path, or busying himself with tucking the ends of his scarf into his coat.

"I've been ill. That's why I'm not back at school," he said. "I have to be careful. I had the flu very badly."

"So did I."

"I don't mean just a feverish cold," he said. "That's what most people mean. I nearly died."

"So did I."

He looked at her disbelievingly. Obviously he thought only the upper classes had the flu; common people merely had common colds. "I'm not strong," he said. "I expect I'll die young."

"I wouldn't be at all surprised."

"Now you're laughing at me," he said. He smiled, looking much younger. Much nicer. If he weren't so pale and thin, he'd be very good-looking, she thought.

"You don't know what it's like," he said. "They're always fussing over me. I'm the only son. The only child left now. If I die, all this" — he waved his arm as if to conjure up the house and grounds in all their splendor, although all Emily could see now were some tattered evergreens — "all this would come to an end. The end of the line. There'd be no more Mallertons at Mallerton House."

"Oh dear," said Emily politely.

"Mother'd like to wrap me in cotton wool and keep me in a drawer till I'm old enough to marry and have a son."

"You'd suffocate."

He looked at her suspiciously. "Are you laughing at me again?"

"Well . . . you do worry about funny things. Why care what happens to the house when you're dead? I wouldn't!"

"You don't understand," he said haughtily. "I suppose one could hardly expect you to."

"No," she said honestly. "I've never met anyone like you before."

He stared at her then.

"Isn't that odd," he said, half under his breath, "because I've met someone like you. When I was so ill, it was your face I saw. Always your face. Staring at me from the shadows. I knew what you wanted. I think I've always known . . ."

"Come off it!" she said uneasily. "It wasn't me."

"No, of course not," he said, in a more ordinary tone. "It was only a nightmare. I know that. I'm not mad." (She was relieved to hear it. She had begun to think he was.) "Only it's so strange, seeing you . . . I feel like Frankenstein."

"Frankenstein?" Then, indignantly, "I'm not a bleeding monster!"

"Yes, you are!" he said, laughing, and looking like a normal boy for the first time. "You're my monster! A monster in a silly army jacket!"

He dodged away as she lunged at him. She gave chase and they ran in and out of the evergreens, laughing and whooping in the cold air. Then Emily, racing round a fir tree to try to head the boy off, found herself on a wide gravel walk, and there, on the other side of a low balustrade, was the lake.

It looked peaceful and innocent. The sun was still out, and on the far side some trees leaned over their red and gold reflections. Three ducks, moving steadily, trailed their wakes like bright streamers across the dark water. She saw patches of vivid green weed and the dark circles of water-lily leaves, though the flowers were long gone.

"Come on!" said the boy. "Why are you stopping? Do you give up?" Then, seeing where she

45

was looking, he said slowly, "Oh, the lake, of course." He came and sat on the balustrade by her side. "I suppose you want to hear what happened?"

"Not if you'd rather not talk about it," she said, trying not to sound disappointed.

"Oh, I don't mind. It won't upset me or anything. It was ages ago. I'll tell you if you like."

But he was silent, gazing over the water, and she did not like to prompt him.

"See that boat?" he said finally, pointing.

She looked and saw a rickety landing-stage, gray with age. At first she could not see the boat at all, then she realized it was half submerged in the water, with reeds growing up all around it and some coming through the planks at the bottom.

"Of course, it wasn't like that then," he said, "although it did leak. We'd been warned it wasn't safe. Someone was supposed to repair it, but nothing ever gets done here. It was summertime, the water lilies were in flower. She wanted to pick some, but you can't reach them from the bank. They're too far out. She said, 'Let's take the boat.' I was very small — she was much older than me — and I hadn't learned to swim yet, so I was . . . not frightened, but . . ."

"I'd have been frightened," said Emily kindly. "If I couldn't swim, you wouldn't get me near a boat."

"Sylvia was never frightened. She was very strong, very brave. She could do anything. She lifted me in. Told me not to be silly. I sat there clutching the seat. I wanted to help her row, but my hands were too small — I couldn't handle the heavy oars. She pushed me away, saying she'd do better on her own. When we got among the water lilies, she passed the oars to me and told me to hold the boat still while she reached for one. I didn't know what she meant — how to do it, I mean. The oars were so heavy and slippery, and when she leaned over, the boat rocked and — and moved away."

He paused, looking sideways at Emily, who sat spellbound, her eyes wide and horrified.

"What happened?" she asked.

"She fell in, of course. Her feet came up and there was a great splash, and I was nearly thrown off my seat. I held on to the oars and waited. I wasn't worried. I knew she could swim. I just worried about keeping the boat from drifting away. I expected any moment that her head would appear over the side. I wondered if she'd be laughing — she never minded getting wet or dirty. Or if she'd be cross with me for not holding the boat still."

"It wasn't your fault!" said Emily, quickly.

"No. No, that's what they all say," he said. "I sat there waiting for her but she didn't come. I suddenly felt I was alone and I was frightened. I looked over the side of the boat, and there she was. I could see her face underneath the water, between the lily leaves. Her eyes were staring at me and her arms reaching up. But her hands were under the water and moved the way weeds do. She was too deep; the weeds held her down. I didn't know what to do. I leaned over the side and tried to reach her but my hand didn't even touch the water and the boat rocked. It was leaking, too — I could feel the water cold on my legs. I screamed. I screamed for help, but nobody came. I just sat there in the sinking boat, looking down over the side. She seemed to hold out her arms, as if — as if she wanted me to join her."

Emily could not speak. While he had been talking, she had seen it all so vividly. Only the little boy in the boat had been her own brother. It was Tim struggling with the heavy oars, Tim's frightened little face looking over the side of the boat.

And she herself was in the dark water, the weeds wrapped around her, holding her to the bottom . . . her arm reaching up, the pale fingers clutching at nothing . . .

She *had* seen that! It was the painting her father had done of her while she was ill, with her hair darkened, as if wet, and one arm, pale as bone, reaching out of a whirlpool of tumbled green sheets! What had made him paint it like that — as if she were drowning!

Oliver was watching her, an odd little smile on his face.

"You know, sometimes," he said, "sometimes I think she is still waiting for me. I hear her voice at night, calling . . ."

6

Kevin sat on the low wall outside the Fairview Hotel, biting his thumbnail. He was frowning, as if he didn't like the taste, and staring up the empty street.

"Oh, where's that silly little beggar gone?" he muttered.

It was dark. She'd miss her dinner if she didn't look out. The steak would be all gone and the fish pie was terrible. Serve her right! He sighed. He rather liked the girl. He looked gloomily at his watch and wondered what to do if she didn't come back at all.

He paid no attention to the car until it started slowing down. Then he stared, leapt quickly to his feet, and had the door open before the car had properly stopped.

Emily, sitting in the back, looked pleased with herself, and this made him cross. He caught hold of her arm and jerked her out of the car while she was still in the middle of thanking the chauffeur.

"Come on, stupid! Your dad's been on the lookout for you. He's just about ready to blow his top. You'll get us both into trouble, you will!"

He pulled her toward the side entrance, and still the silly girl hung back, waving goodbye to the chauffeur.

"Come on!" he said furiously.

"I must thank him properly. Wasn't it kind of him to bring me back? Did you see his uniform? He called me Miss Emily."

"My, aren't we grand!" he said, pushing her through the side door.

"I've had such an exciting time. You'll never guess where I've been."

Won't I just, he thought, but said aloud, "Come on, quick, off with my coat and hood."

"I've such a lot to tell you," she said, her eyes bright, standing meekly like a small child while he pulled off the jacket and hood he had lent her. "Ow, that was my hair!"

"Well, you might help," he said crossly. "And where's my goggles?"

She looked dismayed for a moment, patting her pockets as if so large an object could possibly fit in them.

"I must've left them behind!" She cheered up again. "I can fetch them tomorrow. He's asked me to go riding with him. And to stay to lunch."

She looked at him sideways, wanting to be asked who had invited her to go riding and to stay to lunch, but he wasn't going to oblige. He knew. He'd recognized both the car and the driver.

"Hurry up," he said, taking her anorak out of the cupboard where they had hidden it behind some cardboard boxes. "Get this on."

"Aren't you going to ask me who?" she said, putting it on obediently.

"No."

She looked disappointed.

"Oh, all right. Who?" he asked wearily.

"Oliver Mallerton of Mallerton House," she said grandly.

"Well, now! The little lord of the manor himself!"

She looked at him, some of the pleasure fading from her face. "Why do you say it like that?"

He turned away without answering.

"I suppose you think I'm a snob?"

Shrugging, he opened the door and glanced up and down the street.

"Come on," he said. "Out of here and in again at the front — and I hope you've thought up a story for your dad."

"I'm not a snob, honest," she said. "Only — I've never met anyone really posh before. So it's sort of — interesting."

"Yeah."

"Like being asked out by a dinosaur."

She was trying to make him laugh. Stony-faced, he told her to get a move on. It was late. He wanted his supper, even if she didn't want hers. He had a lot of homework to do.

"Won't I see you later?" she asked, looking like a kid who'd had her lollipop taken away. "I've such a lot to tell you. I've been looking forward to telling you all the way back in the car. I heard such a terrible thing! And I can't very well talk to Dad about it, can I? Not without giving myself away."

He relented, and they arranged to meet in the hotel lounge after she'd had her dinner. He was, to tell the truth, very interested to hear about Oliver Mallerton. There were things he could tell her about that young gentleman if he chose. But he wouldn't, he thought, shutting his mouth in a determined line. There was such a thing as loyalty.

In the hotel dining room, Emily sat opposite her father, wondering whether to tell him she had followed him. After all, what could he do? But the trouble was, she knew only too well what he could do: he could lose his temper, and shout.

She glanced round the room. Two old ladies daintily eating ice cream. A man drinking coffee and reading the evening paper. The waitress yawning behind her hand, wishing them all gone.

Her father never minded having an audience when he lost his temper. She did. It put her in the weaker position, which was unfair, because it wasn't altogether her fault. Why did he have to make a mystery of everything? If he'd said straight out he wanted an afternoon on his own, doing the things he liked doing for a change, she'd never have thought of spying on him. Spying. It was a shabby, furtive word.

She sighed. He looked up from his plate.

"Another time when you're going to be late,

you phone me and let me know," he said. "I was worried."

"Yes. You told me. I've already said I'm sorry. Twice."

"We missed the steak," he complained, looking gloomily at his plate.

"I'm *sorry!*"

"All right, Emily, I won't go on about it anymore. I'm glad you had a good day. So you're off riding with your new friend tomorrow — you've never ridden before, have you?"

"Yes, I have." (Donkeys on Hampstead Heath — she hoped there wasn't too much difference. She hadn't liked to tell Oliver she couldn't ride.) "Anyway, he's going to lend me a proper hat."

"Ah, good. That'll save me from having to buy one. What's his name, by the way?"

The question came too soon; she hadn't decided what to tell him.

"It's — um — it's — oh, a bone!" she said, putting her fingers to her mouth to remove it.

"Owen Bone? Is he a local lad, or just here on holiday? What's the joke, Emily? What are you laughing at?"

"Nothing," she said, wiping her eyes on her

hand. Then, to distract him, "Did you have a good day, Dad? How was Bournemouth?"

"Bournemouth?" he said blankly.

"I thought you said you had business there!"

"Oh, *Bournemouth!*" He examined the grayish lump on his fork thoughtfully. "I suppose this fish pie is all right? No, darling, it wasn't in Bournemouth, it was just outside."

So he wasn't going to confess either!

"How did your business go? Was it a success?" she asked slyly.

"No, the man was out," he said. "It was a waste of time. Still, it wasn't important. I'll just have to wait."

She stared. That had sounded like the truth, somehow. Had he really had business at Mallerton House, after all?

"Will you try again?" she asked, seeing all sorts of complications ahead. But he said no, he might give the fellow a ring sometime. He'd take his paints out tomorrow, if it was fine. He'd deliver her at her friend's house —

"No!" She said it too violently, and he looked at her in surprise while she tried to think of an excuse.

"I hope you're not ashamed of me, Emily, in front of your fine new friend?" he asked gravely.

"*No!* It's not that!"

He waited.

"I just don't want him to think I'm treated like a baby, that's all! He's thirteen. It's perfectly respectable, honestly. They've got a nice house and two ponies and a big garden — *please,* Dad. Mum lets me go everywhere by myself."

He was silent for what seemed like a long time. Then he said he supposed it was all right, only she was to be sure to give him the address before she went.

Now Kevin and Emily had the lounge to themselves. The old ladies were in the television room, and Mr. Dodd was playing bar billiards. The children were laughing over Mr. Dodd's mistake.

"Just when I was on the point of confessing," said Emily.

"What about an address for him? Owen Bone, address unknown," said Kevin, finding this very funny.

"Oh, he'll probably forget to ask for it. He's not a worrier like Mum. We can always get round him —" She stopped and looked shamefaced. "Poor old Dad. I feel a bit mean."

57

"Too easy, was it?"

"He trusts me. I wish I'd told him now."

"I'd leave it be," said Kevin. "He wouldn't like being spied on — nobody would! Whether they'd been up to anything or not."

"He wasn't up to anything!" Emily said quickly.

"Never said he was, did I? Don't fly out at me, Titch."

"It was . . . I did it for a dare."

"Ah, that'll be it," he agreed, his eyes disbelieving. "So he landed up at Mallerton, did he?"

"He *enjoys* looking round stately homes. He and Mum often do it."

"Ay, there's lots of folks like it," said Kevin, soothingly, "though not at this time of year, maybe. It'd be a small party going round?"

"I didn't risk it. I went to the Maze," said Emily, glad to get away from the subject of her father and on to her story.

She told it well. As she spoke, she was back on the balustrade again, looking over the dark water, the wind cold on her face, the boy's tale cold in her ears.

Kevin listened silently. Only an occasional

raised eyebrow or twitch of his lips indicated that he could, if he chose, tell a very different tale indeed.

"The boat was sinking," said Emily, coming to the end. "He screamed and screamed, but nobody came . . ."

"Poor little boy," said Kevin, shaking his head solemnly and exchanging a glance with the ceiling. "So he drowned?"

"Of course he didn't!" said Emily irritably — and then she said it, using the same careless tone Oliver had used. "Some servant's boy heard him and fished him out."

Kevin flushed a dark red. Emily, astonished, thought for a moment he was about to burst into tears. But his eyes were dry. He picked up the poker and started attacking the fire as if he were trying to kill it dead.

"What's the matter? What is it? What have I said?" she asked, dismayed.

"Some servant's boy!" repeated Kevin bitterly. "Has he forgotten my name, then? Has he forgotten we was friends once? Bloody little snot! He might've given me a name!"

Kevin's mother used to work at Mallerton House as a maid, he told her, and glad she was to get the job. It was not easy for a woman with a child and no husband to go with it.

"I'm a bastard," he said, looking at Emily to see how she'd take this. She took it calmly. Encouraged, he went on. "My dad was a gyppo. Worked the coconuts at the fair — only he moved on before he had time to hear I was on the way. Dunno if he'd have been interested. Dunno if Mum ever tried to chase him up. She wouldn't say. Perhaps she was glad to see the back of him."

"Didn't you ever think of looking for him? When the fair came back? When you were old enough, I mean," asked Emily.

Yes, he told her, once. He and Oliver had been only seven at the time. They'd slipped out and taken a bus to Corfe, where the fair was. They weren't supposed to go, of course. Dirty, rough, thieving lot of people you found at fairs, using language not fit for Master Oliver's little ears. They had no money to spend on merry-go-rounds or bumper cars. Oliver was as short of money as he was, and a toffee apple was all they could manage between them, unless they were prepared to walk home.

So they'd wandered about, looking at all the men, trying to find Kevin's father. Oliver kept pointing to all the freaks, the dwarf who ran the ball pitch, the humpback outside the ghost train.

"There's your father!" he'd say, pointing to a man with a belly like a breadbasket and a head like a billiard ball. "He's the very image of you," and they'd collapse into shrieks of laughter. Oh, they'd had fun, for all they were hot and thirsty.

Then Kevin had seen a man, bare to the waist and brown as a nut, with long curling black hair and a single gold earring. (As he said this, his hand went up unconsciously to touch his own.) They had followed him, staring. Until, outside a caravan, he'd turned and sworn at them, telling them to be off or he'd set the dogs on them, and they'd been frightened and run away.

"Oh, Kevin," said Emily. "Didn't you tell him?"

"A' course not!" said Kevin scornfully. "Probably wasn't my dad at all. Proper fool I'd have looked, flinging myself in his arms! I didn't care, anyhow. Didn't care then and don't care now! Don't you go feeling sorry for me," he added, turning accusingly on Emily.

"I'm not," she said, untruthfully.

"You know something? Oliver's got a family tree like a bloody great oak — only upside down," he said. "And what's he? A piddling acorn on the end of a twig, that's all he is, for sure. Now my family tree ben't begun yet, but when it is, who'll be at the top, eh? Me!" he said proudly, pointing to his chest. "Me. And there'll never be nobody above me, see?"

Emily nodded, much struck by this idea.

"We didn't half catch it when we got back," he went on. "We was late, we missed the bus, and then Oliver had to go and tell them where we'd been. Nanny blamed me, a' course. Nanny always did. Not that I was allowed to call her Nanny, not to her ugly old face, that is. I did once, it slipped out, and she soon put me to rights. 'Miss Pritchard to you, my boy. *You're* not a son of the house. It's a privilege your being allowed to play with Master Oliver, and don't you forget it.' Oh, she wouldn't have had Mum and me in the house, if it had been up to her, the old witch! But they was short of staff. Couldn't get no one to stay out there, too lonesome. And Lady Mallerton stuck up for me."

"What's she like?" asked Emily.

"Oh, a nice enough lady. Bit feeble, but kind. She used to say it was good for Oliver to have a little playmate. It was lonely for him in that big house, she'd say. She thought I was a nice little boy," he said, grinning at Emily. "I wasn't so rough then. My hair was shorter, and I spoke better, too. Caught it off Oliver. Now I don't care. If I come to drop an aitch, I let it lie on the floor. I ben't stooping down to pick up no aitch, not for nobody!"

"What about his sister?" Emily asked, for Kevin had spoken as if there were no other child in the house. "Didn't she play with you? Or did she die before you came?"

"His sister?" said Kevin, looking at her and shaking his head. "Oh, Titch, you han't half been taken in! You don't want to go believing all you're told. Not when it's young Oliver what's telling the tale. Oh, he's full of fancies, that lad. He never had no sister."

"What!"

"Honest, Titch. He's an only child. Ask my mum."

Emily was astonished. She couldn't believe Oliver had been lying. He'd been really frightened when he first saw her. And the woman at the lodge, too, had stared, taking her for someone else.

"But — who is Sylvia?" she asked, confused.

"Sylvia! I hoped I'd never hear that name again! Nor see that face! Lord, you give me a turn, Titch, when I first saw you. You was going into the dining room with your dad, and you turned your head and looked at him over your shoulder — and 'twas her face! If it ben't Sylvia come after me, I thought. I tell you, Titch, it put me right off you at first, the way you look. That's why I was a bit horrid, till I come to know you."

"Who *is* she?"

"Sylvia Mallerton, what drowned in the lake when she was nobbut twelve years old, all among the water lilies, just like he said. Only 'twas a hundred years ago, long afore he was born. There was a picture of her in the gallery, all in white, standing sideways on, looking over her shoulder — with your face, Titch, and your orange hair falling down her back."

"A painting!"

"She should've stayed that way," he said bitterly. "It was that Nanny's fault, horrible old witch. I really thought she was a witch then — a' course, I was only small. She was always telling us about Mallertons what died young. Proper old misery, she was. And little Sylvia was her favorite. You should've heard her!" He put on a high, cracked falsetto and said, "'Oh, the poor pretty little love, lying there among the water lilies, and her face the fairest flower of them all.' Silly old cow!" he went on in his own voice. "How come she knows? She's as old and ugly as sin, but she ben't a hundred yet. And you know what she used to say to Oliver?"

Emily shook her head.

"She'd say — and to him what's always been a bit sickly, catching colds like most boys catch balls — she'd say, 'Oh, this is an unlucky house for children like you.'"

"Why, that's what the woman at the lodge said to me!"

"Ay, you'll have met her. They tried to pension her off but she wouldn't go. So now she lives in the lodge and sells tickets at the gates — with her sour old face putting all the gawks off, I'll bet."

"Gawks?"

"Tourists. People what come to look round the house."

"Oh, thanks!"

"Not you, Titch," he said, teasingly. "You belong there, with your face. Hanging in a frame, or down in the lake with all them water lilies. Best be careful when you go tomorrow, or that's where they'll put you."

"I shan't go!" she said, all her sympathies with Kevin, although she could not help wondering about her striking resemblance, and if perhaps her great-grandmother, the one who'd come from Corfe, were not another little acorn on the great family tree. "I'll let that lousy snob wait, all ready with another pack of lies." But somehow this was not satisfactory. "No, I will go," she decided, "and I'll tell him to his face what I think of him! I'll push him in the lake and see how he likes that!"

"Oh, don't you do that, now!" said Kevin. "He's been in that lake already. It was him and me in the boat what sunk. It was him what got caught in the weeds. We was playing the Sylvia Game."

8

The Sylvia Game. It sounded harmless, not like a game that would nearly cause the death of one boy and lead to the banishment of the other. Two small boys in a large, lonely house, inventing an imaginary companion, choosing from the long line of portraits in the gallery Sylvia Mallerton, the girl who had drowned in the lake when she was only twelve.

"She was always wet," said Kevin. "That had to be part of it. 'Excuse me, Sylvia,' we'd say, 'you've gone and got a poor little goldfish tangled up in your hair.' We was only kids," he added, catching sight of Emily's face. "You couldn't expect us to cry over her. It was just a game."

They'd tell her off for dripping water all over the polished floors, pretend to pluck weeds from her invisible skirts and frogs from her ears. Any mud or mess they brought into the house, they'd blame on her.

"Sylvia did it! It wasn't us! It was Sylvia!" they'd claim, pointing to an empty chair, until the grownups got thoroughly sick of it.

Lady Mallerton wanted them to stop playing the game; thought it was morbid. But Kevin's mother, down in the servants' hall, said it was only natural. Boys would be boys, and anyway, it was that Nanny, filling their heads with her stories.

For nearly three years, the imaginary girl presided over their games. Sometimes as their older sister, sometimes as a princess, she'd sit, wringing the water from her wet white skirts and issuing imperious commands. Or so Oliver said.

"The things she'd have us do!" said Kevin. "Dangerous! I tell you straight, I wouldn't do them now, not if you paid me! See these scars?" He rolled back his sleeve to show her the thin white lines on his brown arm. "Got those falling through the conservatory roof. And that 'un" — he showed her the palm of his hand — "that's when we tried to kidnap old Farley's peacock. Got him in the old tennis net — peck! He fair skewered my hand! Then there was the time I had to tie red ribbons on the horns of Blair's bull . . ."

"Didn't Oliver do anything?" asked Emily indignantly. "Why did it have to be you all the time?"

"Oh, he took his turn, fair enough. Only I couldn't never think up anything fancy like that. Only ordinary things, like climbing trees or scrumping apples. He was the one with ideas."

"And you were the mug who carried them out."

"It was a dare, see? If you didn't do what she said, she'd come and get you in the night. She used to creep out of her picture frame when the house was asleep and go down to the lake to lie among the water lilies. But if you refused a dare, she'd come back and tap on your window — like this!" He knocked softly three times on the wall beside him. "So's you'd know she was coming for you. Then, next minute she'd be there, leaning over the bed, all white and staring. She'd spill dirty water over you, and toads and dead fish. She'd bind you up tight with weeds so you couldn't move, and stuff your mouth with mud so you couldn't scream ... The times I lay in my bed, with the sheets up to my eyes, listening to a branch on the window, tap ... tap ... tap."

"The little beast!"

But he shook his head. He had forgotten his

anger; his face showed nothing but old affection and amusement. He was a good friend to have, thought Emily. She could never forgive anyone who'd spoken of her like that! Never!

"It was only the game," he said tolerantly. "Funny thing," Kevin went on, "he frightened himself most. He come to believe it. Many a night he'd wake up screaming — 'She's coming for me! She's coming for me!' Annie said it made her blood run cold to hear him."

"Annie?"

"Annie Larkin, the upstairs maid. I slept in the servants' wing, see, so I never heard him myself. Fair curdled her blood, she said. Poor old Oliver. Mum always said they'd drive him mad between them. That old witch with her tales, and Lady Mallerton fussing over him every time he sneezed, and Sir Robert trying to make a man of him."

He paused for a moment, gazing into the fire, then said, "D'you think you can *make* things happen? Just by saying them, by thinking them hard enough — like you sort of created them?"

"No," said Emily. But she remembered Tim had been afraid you could — claimed that their father had told him so.

"That's what I said when he asked me. No, I said, that's silly. But — he always said as how she was awaiting him. Down in the lake. She damn near got him in the end."

The last time they played the Sylvia Game was in the summer holidays. When he was eight, Oliver had gone away to his prep school, and Kevin to the local primary. Before that, they had both been taught at Mallerton House by a Miss Tott, who'd come in the mornings. Kevin's mother had not been happy about this, thinking it would be harder for Kevin later, joining the primary as a new boy when all the other kids had been together for years, but she'd been talked round.

"Don't go thinking you and Master Oliver can be proper friends," she'd warned Kevin. "You're useful to them now he's got nobody else. But once he goes off to his posh school, he'll make friends with his own kind, and then it'll be 'Clean my shoes, Kevin!' or 'Oil my cricket bat!' or 'You fetch the balls while I play tennis with little Lord What's-it.' He'll drop you, son. He'll not mean to, but that's the way the world goes. The more shame on us all for it!"

Kevin had not believed her.

"And it wasn't like that," he said. Then, catching Emily's eye, he flushed a deep, painful red, remembering, as she did, Oliver's cruel, careless words. "No, it wasn't, not then!" he said defiantly. "He was pleased to see me. He was jumping with joy to be back at Mallerton!"

Oliver had not said much about his new school. Kevin had got the impression he was unhappy there. Certainly he was delighted to be back home again. They had spent the long, dusty summer days together, and it was just as it had always been, except that they had not played their old game. Not until the last day, when Oliver had suddenly said he wanted to say goodbye to Sylvia.

"We'll take the boat out to the lilies," he'd said. "That's where she'll be, lying at the bottom with the fish swimming in and out of her eyes."

Kevin had been unwilling. He had grown out of the game; it was kid stuff. Besides, it always landed him in trouble. He pointed out that Oliver was wearing his new trousers and Nanny would skin him if he got them wet and muddy. But it was no good. Oliver had his way. He always did.

It was Kevin who had rowed out to the water lilies, he who had handed the oars to Oliver, telling him to keep the boat steady — and Oliver who had jerked the boat, so that Kevin had fallen in.

"He was laughing. He done it on purpose, a' course. He stood up in the boat, holding the oars and calling out, 'Look out behind you, Kevin! She's coming for you!' So I grabbed hold of the oar and pulled him in too. I didn't see why I should be the only one to get wet. But — but he got caught in the weeds! It must've been just the weeds, mustn't it? I thought I'd never get him free, thought we'd both drown! It was like something — someone — was holding him down. But I got him in the end. I won!"

It was a doubtful victory. Oliver had been ill for weeks. The water had got in his chest and he'd nearly died. Kevin and his mother had been asked to leave.

"But you saved his life!" said Emily. "How *could* they? Didn't you tell them it was Oliver's fault?"

"It was that Nanny," Kevin explained. "She always blamed me for everything. Mum and her, they had a terrible row about it. It ended up with Nanny saying either we left or she would — and a' course, she'd been there forever. She'd been Sir Robert's nanny when he was little, see? So it had to be us. They was nice about it — said how they was sorry. Lady Mallerton kissed me and said I was a brave boy. And Sir Robert gave me a fiver and paid Mum's wages for a month. But we had to go."

"Didn't Oliver do anything? Didn't he try and stop them?"

"He was too ill. He didn't know nothing about it at the time."

"But later — didn't you get in touch with him after you left?"

"No," he said. "I got my pride."

"And didn't he ever write?"

"No," he said briefly. But it was obvious he had been deeply hurt.

She said hotly, "Oh, I *am* looking forward to telling that snob just what I think of him!"

"Don't you go saying nothing!" Kevin said, sounding angry. "I wish I never told you! I don't need nobody fighting my battles, thank you! You leave it be. Besides — he was my friend once."

Emily looked at him with enormous admiration. She was not equal to such heights of friendship. *She* could not forgive him! Not only because he'd made a fool of her (she remembered how he'd watched her with the sly smile she'd taken for nerves), but for Kevin's sake. She liked Kevin. If he'd be her friend, *she*'d never let him down.

Later, as she was going to bed, she turned her head and caught sight of herself in the mirror. The glass was a little smeary and the face looked back at her, as if through water; a pale face with large, staring eyes and orange hair falling over the shoulders. *Sylvia!*

"What's happening? Who am I?" she thought, feeling dizzy, as if she were dissolving into someone else before her very eyes.

Then she shook herself.

"I'm Emily Dodd," she said firmly, climbing into bed and pulling the covers up to her nose. "I'm Emily Dodd, daughter of a poor but honest painter."

As she drifted to sleep, her mind filled with what she'd heard, she suddenly seemed to smell oil paint and turpentine, and a half memory tugged at her. But then it was gone again, and she slept.

9

The morning was bright. In the bus, Emily sat gazing out of the window, her lips moving silently. She was rehearsing: "Oh, hullo, Oliver. I think it's only fair to tell you right away that I think you're a stinking snob!"

Honest, perhaps, but as a beginning, it invited too quick an end. A door slammed in her face. A long, lonely walk down the drive. A two-hour wait for the next bus back to Swanham Bay. No ride. No lunch. Nothing.

She sighed, her breath forming a cloudy circle on the glass, dimming her view of the sunlit fields passing by. She drew a face into it with her finger, the nose long and aristocratic, the mouth turning down sadly.

"I'll make you sorry, see if I don't!" she muttered, adding some overlarge tears to its cheeks.

She could have been with Kevin now. His teachers were on a one-day strike, and he was going down to the market to see if any stallholder wanted a hand. He often helped there. They all knew him.

"I might've asked you along," he'd said, "if you wasn't going to Mallerton. Might've given you a share of my earnings. A *small* share," he'd added cautiously.

She wished now that she had gone with him. Her crusading spirit had cooled during the night. Kevin hadn't wanted a champion. "Leave him be," he'd said. "He was my friend once."

Some friend! she thought, prodding her anger back to life.

Goodbye, Oliver. Thanks for the ride and the lovely lunch. (Roast chicken? Strawberries out of season?) And now let me tell you what a louse you are. Serve him right! SNOB, she wrote underneath the face; then wiped her hand over it, only to see through the cleared glass, apparently refusing to be rubbed out, Oliver's face. He was standing on the grass, waiting for her. Behind him, tethered

77

to a rusty ring in the wall, were two horses, one brown, one gray. The bus stopped.

"Hullo," he said, smiling as he came forward to meet her. "I'm so glad you could come." Very polite.

He seemed a different boy today. The tearstains and dirt had been washed from his face, leaving it calm and assured. His riding clothes looked expensive. His fair hair gleamed sleekly in the sun. He looked very much the young aristocrat, and it made her feel shy.

"Oh, hullo," she said, and looked away from him toward the horses. It was a mistake. From close quarters, they looked enormous.

"How'm I expected to get up?" she asked gloomily. "Got a ladder?"

"I thought you said you could ride."

"So I can. Bicycles and donkeys."

"Oh, you'll be all right," he told her cheerfully. "Poor Belle's very lazy now. She's just a fat old armchair."

His face looked too innocent and friendly to be true. What tricks was he planning to play on her? Probably the saddle wasn't fastened properly, she thought uneasily as he led the gray horse toward her. Or perhaps he'd put a thistle under it. No doubt it was part of the Game to humiliate visitors.

"Don't you want to ride?" he asked, watching her. "We can do something else if you like. It doesn't matter."

Like boating on the lake? she thought. No, thanks. Aloud she said she'd like to ride, and he helped her to mount, then left her to unhitch his own horse.

To her relief, the animal on which she sat seemed to have gone to sleep on its feet. But for the twitching of its ears, it might have been stuffed. Encouraged by this, and by the lofty feeling of sitting so high in the sun, she leaned forward and risked an ingratiating pat on its neck. Promptly the creature tossed its head with a jangling of bridle and a scattering of flies, and moved several of its feet. She snatched her hand away. It went back to sleep.

"Come on," said Oliver. "I'll lead the way."

He rode off down the grass. After a moment, her horse, as if realizing it was no use waiting for instructions, started ambling after him. So gentle and unexcited was its manner that Emily was soon able to relax her grip on the saddle and look about her. She found they were in a narrow lane between shaggy hedges. These hedges seemed to have an irresistible fascination for Belle, who walked so close to them that Emily was continually fending off brambles or ducking under low branches. This, and the clumps of grass on which the horse stopped to feed, made conversation rather limited.

Oliver, riding neatly in the middle of the lane, would look back and shout, "Pull up her head! She's fat enough already. Don't walk her into the hedge, silly! Show her who's master."

There was no need: the horse knew.

After a while they left the lane for a wide grass walk, where they were able to ride side by side. The early mist had quite gone and the trees burned orange and gold in the clear light. Oliver showed Emily how to trot, how to rise up and down in the stirrups, missing the alternate bumps.

"Well done!" he said. "That's it! That's very good!"

She smiled at him happily, pleased with his praise, quite forgetting that she disliked him. Even when he called her Sylvia once or twice, she let it go, not wanting to spoil the morning.

This was all their land, he told her. From the top there, she'd be able to see the house through the trees, and the lake . . . He looked at her slyly then, and seemed about to add something. But then he changed his mind and began telling her about his young dog, whom he was trying to train, but who would chase the ducks and fight all the other dogs, making his father angry.

He talked eagerly, almost as if he'd been locked up in a tower for years and was now making up for lost time. Not about Sylvia. No more tales of drownings and ghosts. He spoke of ordinary things: the summer fair that was always held at Mallerton and how angry his father had been at the mess they'd made of his lawns, the dry rot they'd found in the west wing, the local quarry that sometimes had dinosaurs' footprints for sale, how angry his father got with the gawks, who had only to see a notice saying PRIVATE to want to stand and stare through the windows . . .

Emily, listening, noticed how often his father's anger punctuated his speech. Not that he complained. He spoke of his father with admiration. His father was very clever, was never ill, was a fine horseman, setting his hunter at hedges no one else dared attempt. The Mallertons had always been daring riders . . .

"Except me," he added ruefully.

He'd been given a pony for his third birthday, he told her, and it had seemed enormous to him. He'd cried when he'd been lifted onto its back and his father had been ashamed of him.

"I used to dread my riding lessons," he said. "I used to pretend I was ill — say I had a headache or a sore throat. Father guessed I was putting it on. It made him furious. He'd hand me an aspirin or shine a flashlight down my throat to see if it was inflamed, and if it wasn't, I'd have to go. Once I beat my chest with a hairbrush till it was red, and said I had German measles. They called in Dr. Jacobs and Nanny sat with me till he came. Of course it had faded by then. He didn't give me away, though. He said it must've been a heat rash and I should rest and drink plenty of water. And he winked at me as he left the room. He was a good sport."

Emily was surprised to find she felt sorry for Oliver. This was the boy she had envied for his grand home and his titled parents and his wealth! This lonely, pale boy with his fierce father.

"You ride jolly well now," she said.

"Oh, that was thanks to Kevin," he said. "He helped me —"

"Kevin!" repeated Emily. She had never

expected him to bring up Kevin's name. She wasn't ready. She did not want to quarrel on such a bright day. She went on reluctantly, "So you haven't forgotten his name?"

"What do you mean? Of course I haven't! Kevin Dewy's the best friend I ever had. He saved my life once —"

"Yes, you told me. You said — *some servant's boy.*"

"Yes, his mother uscd to work here," Oliver said, apparently puzzled by the emphasis she put on these words. Then, as if he'd thought of a possible reason, he said coldly, "I don't care about that myself. I like people for themselves, whatever their parents are. Are you a snob?"

"Me!" It was too much, having her own accusation spun round like a weathervane to point at her. She exploded. *She* was not a snob! *She* didn't go around referring to her friends as the baker's daughter or the butcher's son, as if they were cards in Happy Families! She gave them their names!

Unabashed, he said it would have spoiled the end of his story.

"You'd have asked me who Kevin was, and I'd have had to explain, just when I was coming to the best bit — you know, where I hear her calling me at night, my poor dead drowned sister. Good Lord, Kevin wouldn't mind! He'd understand it was the Game. Shall I tell you something?" he added, his eyes laughing at her. "Shall I? Shall I own up?"

She had opened her mouth to say Kevin *had* minded, hadn't understood at all, had been hurt, when it occurred to her that Kevin might think this a betrayal — he was a proud boy — so she kept silent. She forgot to shut her mouth, however, and Oliver, obviously thinking he had amazed her, confessed gleefully that he had never had a sister.

"What?" she said, opening her eyes wide, acting surprised.

"I made it all up."

"Really? You did?"

As they rode back to the stables, he told her all about the Game, and she listened quietly, thinking her own thoughts behind an innocent face.

It had been great, he said, they'd frighten any gawk they met in the grounds with tales of drownings, and walking corpses, and man-traps. In wet weather, they used to dress up in sheets and appear briefly at the head of the grand staircase, safe from pursuit behind the red ropes that kept the plebs in their place. Once, when they'd hidden in a cupboard and howled like wolves, they'd heard a father reassure his frightened children, telling them it was not a ghost; it was only the wind in the chimney.

"It's been dull since he left," he said, "boring."

"Why don't you ask him over, then?"

"I don't know where he is," Oliver said gloomily. "There was a row and they left. I missed it all — I was terribly ill. I nearly died." (It seemed to be a habit of his, of which he was rather proud.) "When I was better, they'd already gone and nobody knew where. Father said they'd rushed off without leaving an address."

Emily had seen Kevin's mother bustling about the hotel, a plump woman with sharp smiling eyes. She tried to imagine her sweeping out of Mallerton, her chin held high, her suitcase in one hand, her son in the other, striding out into the dark night and a cold new life. The picture, as her father might have said, was highly colored but lacked conviction. Mrs. Dewy was more likely to have sat on her luggage, folded her arms, and waited to be driven wherever she was going, or she wouldn't go!

Someone was lying, Emily thought. Not Oliver.

85

Not this time. Probably his high-and-mighty father had seized the chance to break up what he considered an unsuitable friendship. Horrid man! What did he care if his son was lonely? Oliver did not seem to have made any friends at his posh school. He was an odd, nervous boy, she thought, as she watched him unsaddle the horses, for they were now back at Mallerton House — he'd make an easy butt for bullies. Probably had a hell of a time, poor devil! Why should he lose the one friend he'd had, just because that friend was a gypsy's son and not a stuck-up, blue-nosed lord?

She smiled suddenly. Why should he? *She* knew where Kevin was.

As they walked toward the house, she said, "Would you like to come into Swanham Bay after lunch? Only there's a splendid street market there . . ."

She'd been afraid he might despise a street market, but to her relief, he agreed readily, seeming pleased with the idea.

"Good," she said.

She did not tell him what she hoped they'd find in the market. With the best intentions in the world, she wanted it to be a surprise.

10

They went into the house through a side door, marked PRIVATE — STAFF ONLY. Emily, following Oliver down a stone-flagged passage, was surprised to see how shabby everything was. The paint was grubby and peeling, the few rugs faded and threadbare. An open door showed a clutter of muddy boots, chewed dog beds, and a row of ancient raincoats on one wall. There was a pervading smell of moldy apples.

Oliver led the way round a corner, down three steps, through a door into a dusty room with a ladder and cans of paint in the middle, into another passage and up three steps ... He was taking her to meet his mother.

"Will your dad be there?" she asked, a little nervously.

"No, he's in London. He's not coming back till late tomorrow."

So her father had been telling the truth. The man was out, he'd said. Why on earth had he wanted to see Sir Robert?

"Is your mother thinking of having her portrait painted?" she asked.

"Not that I know of," he said, looking at her in some surprise. "I shouldn't think so. She's already been done twice. Why?"

He didn't know her father was a painter. Come to that, he knew nothing about her — except that she looked like Sylvia. Far too busy talking about himself!

"I just wondered," she said.

They passed another passage, branching off at right angles. Glancing down it, Emily saw a red rope looped across the far end, and beyond that, a glow of gold leaf, richly colored tapestries, and gleaming wood —

"What's that?" she asked.

"What?"

"Through there."

"Oh, that's only the great hall. You don't want to see that! Come on."

Perversely, now she was on this side of the red

ropes at last, it looked better on the other. Never satisfied, as her mother would say.

"Here we are," said Oliver, stopping. He smiled at her, but she noticed that he gave her a quick, critical glance from beneath his eyelashes, as if wondering for the first time whether she would be considered a suitable friend for him. Whatever his conclusions (and from his expression she did not think they were favorable), he opened the door and stood aside politely to let her pass.

Lady Mallerton was sitting at a writing desk by the window. She looked up as Emily hesitated shyly in the doorway, wishing she'd had a chance to wash her hands and to brush her hair, wishing Oliver had gone first.

"Yes?" said Lady Mallerton. "What is it? What do you want? Are you lost, my dear?"

"Oh, *Mother!* This is Emily," said Oliver, pushing her forward. "I told you about her, remember? The girl I asked to ride with me. She's staying for lunch."

"Oh, my dear, of *course!* How silly of me!" said Lady Mallerton, coming forward to greet Emily. She was a tall woman, with her son's long nose and fair hair, only hers had faded to the color of parchment, and her pale blue eyes were netted with wrinkles. "I thought you were — well, I don't quite know what I thought . . . Did you enjoy your ride? I know you, don't I?" she added, peering shortsightedly at Emily. "We've met before, surely?"

"No," said Emily, and waited for Oliver to point out her likeness to the portrait of Sylvia. To her surprise, he said nothing but, turning away, began fiddling with some things on a little table.

"Do sit down, my dear," said Lady Mallerton. "I just want to finish this letter and then we can talk."

The only armchairs were occupied by sleeping dogs. Emily went toward a small gilded chair . . .

"Not that one, Annabel," said Lady Mallerton. "It's not safe. And *so* precious! We really must get it seen to. Now where did I put my glasses?"

"It's Emily, Mother, not Annabel. And your glasses are there, right in front of you."

She picked them up and, putting them on, looked at her son.

"Darling, you are pale! I hope you haven't overdone things. I don't know what your father will say if . . . He's been so ill," she added, turning to Emily. "This horrid flu . . . My dear, we *have* met!

I'm sure we have. Now, where can it have been? Let me see —"

"I'm starving!" said Oliver loudly. "What's for lunch?"

Emily looked at him curiously. His interruption had seemed deliberate, but she could see no reason for it.

All through lunch, Lady Mallerton talked. A good hostess, she tried to enliven what would have been otherwise a completely silent meal. Oliver, looking sulky, did not open his mouth, except once or twice to put food into it, with no apparent pleasure; and Emily was far too shy to do more than answer direct questions. Lady Mallerton soon established that Emily had a little brother, liked her school, lived in London — so she was here on holiday? How nice! (Emily detected a slight note of relief in Lady Mallerton's voice. She means nice that I'll soon be going back, she thought resentfully.) Meanwhile Lady Mallerton was asking her how she liked Dorset — had her mother taken her to Corfe Castle yet?

"Mum couldn't come. She's at work. Dad brought me."

"And what does your father do?"

"He's a painter," said Emily.

"A painter — my dear, just the man we could do with! We're getting so shabby — just look at that wall! *Black!* The whole place needs doing."

"No, I mean he's —"

"Not that we can afford to have it done this year. It will have to wait. Like so many things. . . . This house simply *eats* money! Oliver, *you're* not eating. I thought you were hungry. Would you prefer an omelette? Yes, my dear, with dry rot and wood-worm and those sinister little things that tick . . . And not a ceiling you can trust! Any morning I expect to wake up absolutely *plastered . . .*"

She paused to give a little laugh, so high as to be almost inaudible to human ears, and Emily, taking her chance, said quickly, "He's an artist."

But it was too late. The conversation had swept past her father. Lady Mallerton looked puzzled.

"Who, my dear? Oliver, you're squinting. Have you a headache?"

It was only the sun shining in his eyes, he said.

"Annabel, my dear, would you mind drawing that curtain behind you —"

"It's *Emily,* Mother."

"Is that far enough?" asked Emily, turning from

the window and glancing over her shoulder at Lady Mallerton, who gave a little shriek.

"Of *course!*" she cried. "No, don't move. Oliver, look! Isn't she the very image of our lost Renoir?"

Lost?

Emily was an artist's daughter. She knew who Renoir was. A French Impressionist, nineteenth century, whose paintings fetched huge sums of money.

"Was it stolen?" she asked.

"*Burnt,* my dear! Burnt to a cinder! Poor little Sylvia, first drowned in the lake and then burnt in the gallery, really, a most unlucky child! And the worst of it was, we didn't get a *penny.* Not a penny! Didn't Oliver tell you about our tragedy?"

"Yes," said Oliver impatiently. How pale he was now! All the color had gone from his face again. Or was it just the shadow of the curtain making him look so odd?

"You didn't tell me about the fire."

"Oh, that's boring!" he said quickly. "You don't want to hear about that!"

But he couldn't stop his mother from talking. Emily learned all about Sylvia, how her mother had been French and had had her painted by

Renoir when they were in Paris. ("Such luck, my dear, when it might've been by just anybody!") She heard about the fire, three years ago now, and how Mallerton might have been burned to the ground had not Oliver smelled smoke and given the alarm; and how the insurance company wouldn't pay up, just because the policy was out of date by a few months . . .

"My fault, my dear! Robert was in America and Mardie — dear Mardie, I don't know how we'd manage without her, she deals with everything — wasn't here either. Her mother was sick, and she had to go home. They kept sending reminders and I kept meaning to see to it, but . . . Poor Oliver was only just recovering from pneumonia. He'd fallen into the lake, the silly boy."

"Oh, do shut up, Mother!" said Oliver rudely.

He was not reproved. His mother merely patted, not slapped, his hand.

"Poor boy, he hates talking about it," she said to Emily.

Emily smiled politely, thinking that if the Dodd flat had caught fire and she'd been the one to give the alarm, saving everybody's life, she would not have minded talking about it in the least. She glanced at Oliver, but he only looked sick and sullen.

Of course, he had lost them both, Sylvia and Kevin. Funny, Kevin had not told her about the fire either! It must have happened about the time he and his mother were chucked out . . . Why hadn't he said anything about it? She frowned, and sat thinking, letting Lady Mallerton's chatter wash over her head. Had Oliver seen anything, anyone? Running down the smoke-filled passages, had he flung open a window to breathe the cold, fresh air, looked out and seen . . . No, I'm being silly! she thought. Mum always says I'm too suspicious.

She shook the idea out of her head in time to hear Oliver say, "No, I'm *not* going to rest on my bed. Don't fuss, Mother! I'm going to Swanham Bay with Emily," and as his mother was about to protest, added to settle the matter, "Father said I was to keep out in the fresh air."

"Well, darling, if your father said . . . You'll look after him, won't you, Annabel?" she said, turning to Emily. "Don't let him get overexcited."

11

The market was crowded. Women holding large shopping baskets and small children stood gossiping in the autumn sunlight, blocking the aisles between the stalls. Emily, darting and pushing and squirming through narrow gaps with the skill of someone used to crowded streets, soon left Oliver behind. She stopped by a china stall, behind which a man stood idly watching an old woman rummage through a basket marked ODDMENTS. 15P ONLY.

"You haven't seen Kevin Dewy anywhere, have you?" she asked.

"Kevin?" he said. "Yeah, 'e's 'elping Bill. Pot plants. Over there, last stall past the fruit and veg."

Emily thanked him and, leaving him to argue with the old woman over a small, lidless teapot, went to look for Oliver. She found him standing gazing wistfully at a secondhand leather jacket with a death's head painted on the back.

"You don't want that," she said firmly.

"Yes, I do."

But he followed her obediently. They passed the fruit and vegetable stalls, and there, behind buckets of tousled chrysanthemums and crisp carnations and hothouse roses, was a stall loaded with pot plants.

It seemed to be unattended. Then a huge rubber plant tottered, moved sideways on the stall, and revealed Kevin, busily polishing its leaves with a cloth.

"Hullo," she said, and waited happily.

He looked up and smiled. Then he caught sight of Oliver and his smile vanished. A brief glance from his dark eyes told Emily just what he thought of her and her bright ideas.

"Look what's turned up," he said. From his tone of voice, it might have been a slug he'd found under a stone.

"Kevin! It's Kevin!" cried Oliver, his face alight with simple happiness. Then he added uncertainly, as Kevin stared back at him with cold eyes, "It is, isn't it?"

"Yes, of course," said Emily, when it became obvious that Kevin was not going to volunteer this information.

"Oh!" said Oliver, laughing. "I thought for a moment . . . It's your hair, it's different. I wish Mother'd let me wear mine like that! Where've you been all this time? Do you live here? Why didn't you ring me?" Kevin did not answer. Oliver, bewildered, turned to Emily and said, "You never told me you knew Kevin!"

"I wanted it to be a surprise."

It had gone wrong. It had been a stupid idea. Stupid!

"A surprise! It's certainly that! Good Lord, this is . . . It's *splendid!*"

Oliver stressed the word as if by doing so he could make it true, looking anxiously at Kevin's unresponsive face. It made him sound like his mother. Affected.

"Oh, *splendid,* old chap! Let's hang out the jolly old flags, shall we?" said Kevin in cruel mimicry.

Oliver flushed.

"It wasn't Oliver's fault," said Emily quickly, trying to put things right. "Your mother never left an address —"

"Didn't she now? That was right careless of her."

"Oh, is that it!" said Oliver, his face clearing. "Kev, you old idiot, you didn't think . . . I asked everyone! Nobody knew where you'd gone! Father said . . ." His voice trailed away, as he realized for the first time that he might not have been told the truth. "You mean, she *did?*"

Kevin shrugged and did not answer. There was a horrid little silence.

Then Kevin said, very nastily, "Well, it's been a treat meeting you again, Master Oliver. Don't let me keep you now. I got work to do."

Emily could have hit him.

"Yes, you have!" she said angrily. "You can sell me a plant! That's what you're here for, aren't you? Come on, boy, show us something."

Kevin looked at her; he picked up a cactus.

"Go on!" said Emily, getting ready to duck. "I dare you!"

But he thrust it toward her face, saying furiously, "Put your nose in that, miss! That'll learn you to keep it out of other people's —"

Then he put the cactus down very quickly.

Turning, Emily saw that a large man had come up and was beaming at them cheerfully.

"Let 'er 'ave it cheap, lad, as she's a friend of yours. Ten p — 'ow's that, missie? Worth thirty p anywhere," he said. Then, as she looked at him speechlessly, he added in a burst of generosity, "Oh, give it to the little lady. Gift of the 'ouse! Wrap it up, lad, and then go off with your mates for summat to eat. I'll take over now. Go on," he said, as they stared at him dumbly, " 'ave a good time. You're only young once. Long as you're back by five, Kev. Don't forget your cactus, miss."

There was nothing they could do but go off together.

They walked silently. Emily in the middle. On one side of her, Kevin, with a huge scowl on his face. On the other, Oliver, pale and haughty, looking like a young Saint Sebastian, stuck all over with arrows and too proud to mention it.

She wasn't going to speak. They could walk to the ends of the earth in silence for all she cared. And beyond. Let them walk into the sea and drown, the stupid creatures!

They came to a café and stopped. Looked at one another.

"You don't have to put up with me any longer," said Oliver, his nose in the air. "I'm going."

"Suit yourself," said Kevin.

"Oh, come on!" said Emily, losing her temper. She pushed Oliver toward the café, catching him off-balance so that he stumbled and, falling against the swing door, shot through it to land on the floor on the other side.

Kevin laughed.

The door was still swinging, and they could hear Oliver's voice, coming through in gusts.

"Sorry . . . tripped . . . No, it wasn't . . ."

"All right, Titch, come on!" said Kevin.

They went into the café. The woman behind the counter said aggressively, "Now you can go right out again. And take your friend with you. I'm not having any trouble here. If you can't behave . . . Oh, it's you, Kevin!"

"Sorry about that, missus," Kevin said easily. "My . . ." But he couldn't bring himself to say "friend." "My mate tripped. Honest! Haven't hurt yourself, have you?" he asked Oliver, who was standing, brushing dust off his clothes, his face red. "Better sit down. You look all shook up."

He pushed Oliver down onto a chair and held him there, with a hand on his shoulder.

"Been ill, he has," he announced to the other customers, who were all staring. Oliver looked furious.

Emily left them to it. She went to the counter and spent as long as possible choosing three doughnuts and three Cokes. She supposed she would have to pay. When she looked over her shoulder, she saw to her relief that they were talking quietly, their heads close together.

That was all right then. Lot of fuss about nothing.

She came back toward the table in time to hear Kevin say, in a low voice, ". . . what Mum can't forgive. Not ever. Didn't you know he put the police onto us?"

They had not noticed her. Emily stood still, the tray in her hands. She listened.

"The police? *Father* did?" Oliver looked utterly astonished. He half smiled, as if he thought Kevin was joking. (No, he hadn't known, decided Emily.)

"After the fire — they thought I done it. For revenge, see?"

"You!"

Oliver's face was dead white. She had never seen a boy who changed color so rapidly and so often. His skin must be as thin as tracing paper.

"Because of Mum's getting the push," Kevin was saying. "Didn't you know they thought it was done deliberate? Arson, they said. Dunno how they tell, but Mum says they can."

Oliver was shaking. He took his hands off the

table and hid them in his lap. He opened his mouth but no sound came out. Kevin looked at him, and looked quickly away.

"It don't matter," he said. "They couldn't prove nothing. I was with Mum all that night, like she told them. Not that they believed her. Thought she'd say it anyway — well, so she would, a' course, but it happened to be God's truth. They was just trying it on for laughs, I expect. Don't suppose they can tell arson from an ass —" He stopped as he saw Emily.

She was staring at Oliver, her eyes wide and unfocused, seeing in her mind a different picture . . . A small boy in pajamas, creeping through the night, his bare feet making no sound on the wooden floor. A boy who had been brought up son and heir to a great house, with all he could ask for, horses, dogs, fountains, lakes — everything money could buy. And something it couldn't: a friend like Kevin.

But it hadn't been enough. Oh no, he'd wanted a ghost as well. So he had made one up out of a painting. Had he come to hate her in the end, the little monster he'd created?

"It wasn't Kevin at all!" she said, pleased with her discovery. "It was *you!* You did it yourself, didn't you, Oliver! You burned Sylvia!"

"No!" He jumped up, knocking the tray out of her hands, so that the doughnuts went flying like soft cannonballs and the bottles of Coke smashed on the floor. "I didn't! I didn't!" he screamed at the top of his voice. "Don't say that! Don't ever say that again or I'll — I'll kill you!"

12

They stood in a doorway, Kevin and Emily shielding Oliver from public gaze while he rubbed at his cheeks with his handkerchief.

"Is that all right?" he asked, showing them his face. "Can people tell I've been crying?"

"No, it's fine," said Emily untruthfully. He seemed calm now. Almost cheerful.

There had been a terrible scene: Oliver screaming like a mad boy, Kevin trying to quieten him, and the proprietress, who had rushed out from behind her counter, hissing as angrily as her coffee machine. Eyes staring. Voices saying, "Slap his face! Throw a bucket of water over him! Put his head down between his knees!" and then, when Oliver had dissolved into tears, becoming kinder and suggesting things like cups of tea and bed and brandy. And her own voice saying, over and over, "I'm sorry. I didn't mean it. I was only joking."

"That's one café we'll never dare show our faces in again," said Kevin.

"It's just because I've been ill," said Oliver. "I mean, it was a sort of breakdown, wasn't it?"

"Sure. It wasn't your fault, mate," said Kevin kindly. "It was hers . . . making stupid accusations like that!"

"Yes," Oliver agreed. "It was Sylvia."

And they turned to look at her, saying, "It was you, Sylvia. You did it!"

"You always blame me," she said, her voice petulant and high-pitched, oddly unfamiliar.

Then she stood, utterly confused, for a moment not knowing who or what she was.

"I'm *Emily!*" she said desperately, trying to get a grip on herself, for she seemed to be sliding away. "I'm not Sylvia, I'm Emily!"

"No, you're Sylvia," they said, smiling slyly.

They were only teasing, she told herself. They didn't mean to be horrid. They couldn't know how unsettled it made her feel. Like her father's portraits of her at home: *The Laughing Girl, The Sick Child* . . . Never *Emily!* When she had been so ill, they had frightened her, these alien children with their borrowed faces, *her* face, looking down at her from the studio walls — critically, as if *she* were the imitation and they the true daughters.

"I'm no oil painting!" she said crossly, and then had to laugh, and they were friends again.

They walked together down the street. The sun had gone and it was getting cold. It was time to part. Kevin had to go back to his stall and Oliver had to catch his bus, for his mother wanted him home early. They lingered on the corner, wanting to say something, but not knowing what to say.

"Ollie, I'm . . ." Kevin hesitated on the brink of apology. "I'm glad Titch brought you along, after all," he said.

"Me, too. Look, you must come . . . Why don't we . . . We must keep in touch," said Oliver. But the shadow of his parents' disapproval fell across his words.

"Yeah. Sure. Let's do that," said Kevin.

It seemed to Emily that they smiled at each other sadly, as if they knew they could never be again the two small boys, close as brothers, who'd played the Sylvia Game through the dusty summers and cold winters at Mallerton.

She felt close to tears. She wanted to go home. Not just back to the hotel, but home to her mother and Tim. She was surprised when Oliver, after Kevin had left them and they were waiting for the bus, asked her to come riding again tomorrow. She had thought he must be feeling as she did. In his place, she'd never want to see herself again.

As she hesitated, he added, "That is, if you'd like to," looking oddly young and anxious, like Tim when he'd asked for a sweet and didn't think he'd get one. How lonely he must be!

"Yes. All right," she said.

"You don't still think I did it, do you?"

"No," she lied.

When Emily got back to the hotel, she found her father in the lounge, still wearing his old painting coat, spattered all over with more colors than a peacock could boast of in its tail. He was showing his new painting to one of the old ladies, with the defensive smile of someone whose work too seldom brought the praise he knew it deserved.

The old lady took off her spectacles and polished them on the end of her long silk scarf. Put them on again and surveyed the painting once more, her head on one side.

"Oh, I *see!* Yes . . . yes, of course. It's very nice. Maybe if you had it framed," she said kindly. "It makes such a difference. I used to paint a little too, when I was a girl. Watercolors. I often wish I'd kept it up. It's nice to have a hobby when you're old." She smiled and nodded and pattered thankfully away.

"Let's see your painting," said Emily.

He propped it up against the mirror. "What do you think?" he asked. She knew he wanted praise more than he pretended, and said quickly, "Oh, Dad, it's splendid!" She would have said so whatever it had looked like. She hated to see him deflated.

He had painted a group of trees, stark against a stormy sky. At least, she thought that was what it was; with her father's paintings it was not always possible to be sure.

"It's powerful," she said (she knew the words of praise he liked; nice was not one of them), "very vigorous! I like the way the colors sort of vibrate. And the spatial harmonies . . ."

"Oh, Emily!" he said, bursting out laughing

and hugging her. "Spatial harmonies, my foot! Where did you get that one from?"

"*Art News,*" she admitted. "But I do like it, honest, Dad."

"That's my kind girl," he said fondly, and then went on to ask her about her day — had she fallen off the horse? Had they given her a good lunch? Was she going to see the boy again — what was his name? Oh yes, Owen Bone, wasn't it?

"No, he was boring," she said, glad to be able to bury that lie. She had prepared a better story to tell him on the way back to the hotel, a cunning patchwork of the truth.

"I went to see Kevin after lunch," she said, "at the street market. There was a friend of his there, a boy called Oliver."

"Oliver," he repeated, but only to show he was listening, not, she thought, because the name meant anything to him. He was studying his painting critically, reaching out to soften a brushstroke with his thumb.

"He asked me to go riding with him tomorrow. I said I would. That's all right, isn't it, Dad?"

Her father turned to look at her. She felt herself flushing, but he was not suspicious. "Pink cheeks, bright eyes, and a cold nose," he said, touching it lightly. "It seems to be doing you good, all this fresh air and horses. Perhaps I should try it someday. Yes, of course you can go, Em."

That evening, when they were coming out of the dining room, Mrs. Dewy stopped Emily.

"If you've got a minute, Kevin would like a word with you," she said, "on the phone. You can take it at the desk if you like, dear."

Emily thanked her and, walking over, picked up the receiver.

"Hullo," she said.

It was a bad line. Through a gentle hissing, Kevin's voice came in a hoarse whisper, unrecognizable, oddly sinister. "Titch?"

"Yes."

"Any big ears near you?"

"Any big what?"

"*Ears!* Anyone listening."

"Oh! No." Mrs. Dewy was talking to her father some way off, and there was no one at the reception desk. "Where are you?" she asked.

"In Bournemouth with my mates. Look, I gotta be quick. You ben't been shooting your mouth off about you-know-what, have you?"

"No, of course not."

"Well, don't. It's a . . ." His next words were lost. She thought one of them was "criminal." "You can go to prison for it," he said. (For what? Arson? Slander?) "You wouldn't want . . ." He broke off and she heard other voices and laughter, and then Kevin again, much louder. "Get out of here, you beggars! This is a private call. Go on, shove off!"

Now the line hissed quietly to itself.

"Kevin?"

"Yes?"

"Who was that?"

"My mates. It's all right, they've gone now. What I wanted to say was — don't you go round making no accusations. Not to nobody, see?" There was a loud crackling, as if the telephone box had caught fire. Then his voice again, saying, "You keep quiet, if you know what's good for you."

"Are you threatening me?" she asked, astounded.

There was an odd sound. The line cleared suddenly and she realized he was laughing.

"Yeah, reckon I am. I'll knock your block off personal if you go round making trouble for — for anyone. It ben't none of your business, see? Titch? Titch? Are you there?"

"Yes."

"Now you're cross," he said accurately. "I done it wrong. Look, I'm sorry. *Please* don't say nothing — is that better?"

"I wasn't going to," she said, still resentful.

"You don't know them Mallertons like I do," he said, sounding relieved. "They hear you been saying things against Oliver, and they'll do you for it. Sir Robert ben't a good man to cross."

13

Oliver was not waiting for her at the gates in the morning; she hoped he had not forgotten he'd invited her. She walked slowly down the long drive, expecting to see him at any moment, round every corner, but he did not come.

The house, sprawled behind its lawns and fountains, looked deserted. Oh well, here goes, she thought, and walked up the steps to the massive front door. She could see neither a bell nor a knocker. She rapped with her fist, but the sound seemed to lose itself in the solid oak. She knocked again, harder, and stood back, sucking her knuckles. She waited. No one came.

She was going down the steps again, despondently, when she heard the door open behind her.

"Hullo, I saw you through the window. Did you

114

ring? I didn't hear the bell." It was not Lady Mallerton. It was a short brisk woman, with soft gray curls and a look of almost childish excitement on her pink face. She stepped through the door and pulled a handle on the end of a rusty chain, disarranging the creeper that had half hidden it. Immediately a loud, metallic clanging sounded through the house. "Oh, good. It *is* working. We don't usually use this door except for the public, but never mind, now you're here . . . No, it's all right, Maria, I was just testing the bell," she said to someone over her shoulder, and then turned back to Emily. "Come in, there's a terrible draft. It's much colder today. That's right, just let me shut the door. I'm Miss Marsden, and you must be . . ." She paused briefly to flick through her memory, and came up efficiently with the right answer. "Emily."

"Yes." They were in the great hall, with its vast oak staircase, its galleries and tapestries, its ormolu, marble, and gilt. There was even a suit of armor, though somewhat small, which a plump, dark-haired maid was busily dusting. "Oliver asked me to come riding . . ."

"Yes. My dear, I *am* sorry. I'm afraid Oliver isn't feeling quite the thing this morning. I expect it's just the excitement, but we think he ought to rest . . . Maria, if you've finished with that polisher, I should unplug it. Someone's going to trip over that cord. Oh, never mind, I'll do it myself. Do you speak Spanish?" she asked Emily, who shook her head, bewildered. "No, nor do I. It makes things very difficult. Never mind, we'll manage. Maria," she said, turning to the maid and speaking loudly and slowly, "will you take this young lady up to Master Oliver, please? Master Oliver."

The young maid nodded and smiled nervously.

"I only hope she remembers the way," said Miss Marsden, turning back to Emily. "Shout if you get lost. You will stay and amuse Oliver, won't you? I know he's looking forward to seeing you. And I'll leave him to tell you our *splendid* news."

With that, she smiled and hurried off.

"Please, you come?" said Maria, and led the way through a maze of corridors, up narrow flights of stairs, and along a passage.

"What's the matter with Oliver?" Emily asked.

"Please?"

"Is he ill? Sick?"

"Not sick, no. He . . ." Maria gestured wildly with her hands. "He . . . go down."

"Down? Down where?"

"He come like everybody when the master shout. He look at her — he say up high, 'Sylvia! No, no!' and he go down on carpet, like so . . ." Maria rolled her dark eyes upward, and swayed as if she were drunk.

"Oh, he *fainted!*"

"Fainted. Yes. It is the true word," said Maria, smiling.

Emily was about to ask more when the maid opened a door onto a large, airy, empty room. Empty, that is, except for a big black dog who pushed past them and ran off down the passage.

"He not here," said Maria, puzzled. "Is right room, I think."

It was a large bedroom, with two armchairs covered in faded chintz, an old scarred and ink-stained desk with brass handles, a new and glossy stereo system, and a great many cupboards and shelves. Against one wall there was a bed, which had obviously been left in a hurry, for one of the pillows and half the bedclothes were on the floor. The maid replaced these, said hopefully to Emily, "Please, you wait, yes? Perhaps he come," and left the room.

Emily could hear her heels tapping away on the wooden floor. Then there was silence.

She looked around. There was an engagement calendar on the desk, and after a brief, losing battle with her conscience, she went over to look at it. There was nothing for today or yesterday, but on the day before was written: "Terrible row with Father re Jasper. He said he'll have him put down if he kills any more ducks, it's not fair! If he touches Jasper when I'm back at school, I'll . . ." The next two lines were heavily crossed out. So that's why he was crying, thought Emily. She read on.

"He is going up to London today and will not be back till Wednesday. I hope he . . ."

Whatever he'd hoped, he had apparently been afraid to commit it to paper, for there was only one more word on the page, written in red ink and underlined three times: SYLVIA.

There was a noise outside. Emily shut the book and moved hastily away from the desk. It was an odd sound: rasping, scraping, panting. She crossed the room quietly and looked out into the passage. At the far end, the black dog was scratching energetically at a door. Splinters of fresh wood lay at its feet.

"You'd better stop that," said Emily, going

toward it. "Poor old boy, have they shut you out, then?"

The dog looked up at her and wagged its tail ingratiatingly.

"Oh, all right!" She opened the door and it bounded up some dark stairs, its claws clicking on the wood, and vanished from sight.

What an odd place to keep a staircase, hidden behind a door! She looked up into the gloom, her mind filling with old tales of madwomen or monsters locked away in attics. She heard the dog barking excitedly, then a voice, high-pitched and thin, "Down, sir! Down, damn you!"

It was Oliver.

She went quickly up the stairs, the noise of her shoes and the creaking of the old wood masked by the frantic yelping of the dog, and came into a large attic. It was lit by a single, unshaded bulb, which cast its dusty light onto a jumble of broken furniture, trunks and packing cases, an old rocking horse with a missing leg and no tail, rolls of mouse-nibbled carpet — and Oliver.

He was standing insecurely on a wobbling stool by a high cupboard, holding above his head a long bundle wrapped in an old yellow sheet, while his dog leaped about him joyfully, convinced against all persuasion that his master wanted to play.

"Down, you brute! Down, Jasper! Down!" Oliver cried.

Jasper, mistaking the order, brought *him* down. Boy and dog fell together, all tangled in yellow cloth, while something long and narrow shot out from the confusion and landed near Emily's feet.

She picked it up. It was a roll of canvas, old, stained, the edges a little ragged as if they had been cut by an inexperienced hand. It was very large — she could not unroll it completely, stretch her arms though she might . . .

"What are you doing? How did you get here? Put that down! It's mine. Give it to me. *Don't look at it!*"

It was Oliver screaming at her, his eyes blazing in his wild white face. He was sitting on the floor, holding his dog by the collar.

"I'll set my dog on you!" he threatened.

It was too late. Emily had seen enough. She had seen a white dress she remembered only too well. A silly, old-fashioned dress with a tucked bodice, a pale green sash, and deep frills laced with ribbons, green and blue. A dress her father had given her over a year ago and bribed her to pose in. How could she have forgotten that pose? She remembered now how her neck had ached as she had stood and looked at him over her shoulder, one hand bent up to hold a strand of her long orange hair, the other holding a hoop . . .

"It's *me!* It isn't Sylvia at all, it's *me!*" she exclaimed, surprise pushing all other thoughts from her head. "That's my dad's painting! The old liar!" She frowned. "He said it had gone wrong and he'd painted it out!"

14

Oliver was trying to get the painting away from her. Emily held on, saying, "No! No, I want to see —"

"Let go!"

"No!"

Now the dog was leaping up at her.

"Call him off!" she cried, frightened, seeing the strong teeth and glistening tongue close to her face. She let the canvas roll up and threw it wildly in the air, hoping the dog would chase it. He did.

Oliver got there first, thrust the canvas into a trunk, and slammed down the lid.

"Come on! Quick!" he said, pushing her toward the stairs.

"The painting —"

"It's all right in there."

"But I wanted to see —"

"Later! Later!" he said. "Do you want to get us into trouble? We've got to get back before they come."

"Who?"

"Oh, *anybody!*" he said impatiently. "All of them! How should I know? They'll be bringing milk and cookies — they mustn't find us here! Come on!"

The stairs were dark. Emily nearly stumbled as the dog brushed past her knees. It seemed to have given up any idea of biting her; indeed, as she paused at the bottom, she could feel something slapping against her legs and realized it was wagging its tail.

"See if the way is clear," Oliver whispered.

"Why me?"

"It's better."

For whom? she wondered. She opened the door carefully, slipped through, and shut it behind her. She was glad to be alone in the empty passage. She needed time to think. Stray memories shifted restlessly in her head, like dust motes dimming a ray of light, making it difficult to see what lay beyond . . .

"Dad, why is the studio door locked?"

123

"Because I'm sick of you kids running in and out as you please, mucking about with my paints . . ."

The white dress, all frills and ribbons, lying in tissue paper — "I hate it! You only bought it because you want me to pose in it!" *The white dress, all frills and ribbons — now on an old canvas in a dusty attic — an old canvas . . .*

The studio door is unlocked. She is standing in front of a faded green sheet, tacked to the wall behind her. The easel is by the window. She can only see the back of the painting — "Dad, what a filthy old canvas! It's all stained!"

"I'm using up an old one."

"Can I see?"

"No. Don't look, Emily! Go away! I want it to be a surprise. I'm trying something new, a different style . . ."

A different style. The answer was there, waiting to be let into her head. She seemed to hear it knocking for admittance; but it was only Oliver, tapping softly on the door behind her.

She opened it. "All right, you can come out. There's nobody here."

"Why were you so long?"

But without waiting for an answer, he ran off down the passage, the soles of his bare feet showing black from the dust in the attic. His dog ran with him, barking.

She followed slowly. By the time she reached his room, he was back in bed, the dog lying beside him, licking his face. She sat down and looked at him.

"He'd better wash your feet too," she said. "They're filthy."

It was not that she cared about his feet. It was merely something to say. She didn't want to talk about the painting. She didn't even want to think about it.

Oliver was watching her. She did not notice that he was trembling.

"You can't tell anyone, you know," he said. He attempted a confident smile; it flickered briefly like a candle flame in a draft, then went out, leaving his face pale and frightened. "You can't ever tell — or I'll tell on your father!"

"What do you mean? You don't know anything about Dad!"

"Yes, I do! I know he's a forger!"

"That's a dirty lie!" she shouted.

But even as she denied it, she thought, *of course!* A forger! Not, as she had sometimes suspected, a thief or a spy; not planning to run off with a model and leave them all . . . How could she have been so silly, when the answer was obvious! Her father, behind the locked studio door, had been cunningly faking Old Masters. Well, it wasn't so bad. It didn't hurt anyone, did it? It wasn't like stealing; it was *giving* something to the world, a new painting, even if under an old and borrowed name. Most people would only laugh . . .

She felt more like crying. She didn't know why. A faker? Her father, who had always said one had to be true to something in this world . . . "With all my faults," he'd so often said (and she and Tim would exchange glances, knowing what was coming), "with all my faults, at least I'm true to my art." Fool that she was, she had believed him. Seen him secretly as some sort of knight, with a paintbrush for a lance and a palette for a shield, riding out cheerfully to fight bills and bailiffs and the men who came to cut off the electricity.

I'm not a baby anymore, she told herself firmly. This is the real, shabby world I live in. I've known for ages Dad wasn't perfect. All right, he's a faker, so what?

"You gave it away yourself," Oliver was saying.

"You know you did! 'That's Dad's painting,' you said!"

"I didn't mean it! I was joking!" she said quickly. "That's an old painting, any fool can see that! The paint's cracking, and . . . and it's not even in his style, it's a different style . . ."

"Don't! *Please,* don't!" said Oliver.

She looked at him in surprise, for he sounded near tears, and she could not think what *he* had to cry about. He was sitting bolt upright in bed, his eyes fixed on her pleadingly.

"Don't pretend!" he said. "Can't you see? It's quite safe! We can tell each other anything, everything. You don't have to lie to me. We're in it together."

She was silent.

"I must talk to someone. I want to tell *someone,*" he said. "And there's no one else. There's only you. *Please,* Emily."

She bit her lip. She, too, felt the need to talk to someone, and who else was there? She couldn't tell Mum. Nor Tim. And she would never get her father to admit the truth. There was only this boy, who had his own secrets to hide.

"All right," she said.

But having got her to agree, he now seemed doubtful. He wanted her promise of secrecy. She gave it. It was not enough. He wanted her hand of honor: they shook hands solemnly. It was still not enough. He hesitated, as if wondering what the honor of a Dodd was worth.

"Swear on your mother's grave . . ."

"Don't be silly, she hasn't got one!" said Emily impatiently. "Anyway, I know your secret. I was right, wasn't I? *You* set fire to the gallery."

He was silent. Then he gave a long sigh.

"Yes," he said simply, and smiled.

She had to smile back. He looked so innocent and trustful, sitting in his bed, with his fair hair tousled and his arm round his dog's neck.

It was because he had been given an archery set for his birthday, he told her. His mother would not let him go out, as it was raining and he had only just recovered from pneumonia. So he'd set the target up at one end of the portrait gallery. It was quite safe. It was a Sunday, when the public were not admitted, and nobody else ever bothered to go there. He was having a wonderful time, until he shot Great-Aunt Margaret . . .

"Straight through the heart," he said. "It

128

would've been a splendid shot if I'd meant it. It's very difficult to get the arrows to go *anywhere*. It wasn't really my fault! It was that damned pug of Mother's. I heard a noise behind me and I must've jerked, just as I let the arrow fly. It tore a great hole in the canvas. I tried to pull the edges together but it just made it worse. The paint kept flaking off. I couldn't tell Father! I couldn't! You don't know what he's like. He'd have killed me. He loves Mallerton so . . ."

More than he loves his son? she wondered.

"It could've been repaired," she said aloud. "You didn't have to burn down the whole gallery."

"I was only nine," said Oliver, wriggling down in his bed, as if trying to look small and pathetic again. "I was only a kid. And I'd been ill — you can't blame me! I've paid for it, oh God, you don't know what it's been like, these last three years! I kept dreaming — *horrible* dreams! The fire — the fire was so quick! That was the paraffin, I suppose. The flames seemed to explode. They leapt toward me. They seemed to chase me as I ran, screaming . . ." He stared at her. In his wide, frightened eyes, she thought she saw the reflection of the pursuing flames. "I thought the whole house would burn down and everybody in it! I thought I was a murderer and I wished I were dead. Oh, but not like that! Not burned alive!"

"It's all right," she said, for he was shaking so much that his dog growled uneasily and glared at Emily. "Oliver, it's over now. It's all over now."

He leaned back on his pillows. Gradually the remembered fear left his face and he looked almost happy. "It's funny. Telling you — I thought I'd never be able to tell anyone — it's . . . it's all right. I don't mind your knowing, somehow. It doesn't seem so . . . I mean, you don't think it's all that bad, do you? And you mustn't worry about your father. We can't tell on each other," he said, putting his thin fingers round her wrist, as if claiming her. "It's our secret now, forever."

There was a pause. Silence. Then the wind blew a branch against the window, tap, tap, tap. Emily looked round nervously, almost expecting to see Sylvia, white and dripping; but there was only the branch and the gray sky.

"It's your turn now," Oliver said. "Go on."

"I — I can't. I don't know anything," she stammered; then, seeing his furious look, she added helplessly, "All right, that's Dad's painting in your attic. It's a fake. But I don't know how it got there, honest I don't!"

To her surprise, he laughed. "Oh, that's not your father's," he said. "That's the Renoir. That's Sylvia. *You're* downstairs in the study." She stared at him blankly and he added, "I couldn't let poor Sylvia burn, could I? It would've seemed like murder. I cut her out of her frame with my new knife — it was quite easy. I only jagged her a little at one corner. Then I rolled her up and hid her in the attic. You didn't guess there were two paintings, did you? Nobody knows except me. Father found the other one this morning. That's what all the excitement was about. Didn't they tell you?"

15

Sir Robert had gone out after breakfast to have a look at the old icehouse (a sort of room built into the ground, where they used to keep ice before fridges were invented, Oliver explained impatiently). His father had some plan to make use of it, as an ice cream kiosk or new lavatories or something. Oliver had not really been listening. His father had wanted him to come along, but he had refused, saying he had to get ready for his ride. Lady Mallerton, who was asked next, had also refused: she had a headache. And Mardie, that was Miss Marsden, who looked after everything, had slipped quickly out of the room, murmuring something about being busy. His father had left in a temper, saying he could never get anyone to show the least interest. Mallerton could fall to pieces for all they cared. Oliver had been glad to see him go.

But Sir Robert had not been gone ten minutes before he was back, shouting in great excitement, calling everyone to come to his study and see what he had found. Everyone had to come, even the servants; he seemed determined to have a large audience for his great discovery.

"Look at this," he had said.

The canvas was spread out on the table, held down at the corners by paperweights and ashtrays to keep it from rolling up. Oliver was the last one to come in, and they made way for him ... And there she was, Sylvia in her white dress! His heart had jumped ...

"It really did, you know," he told Emily. "It was a very odd feeling. I thought it was mine, you see — the one from the attic, I mean. It was exactly the same — the face, the dress, even the old cracks here and there ... I thought they'd found out, that they'd guessed ... So I fainted." He said this with the air of one who had known unerringly the right thing to do.

When he came to, he was lying on the sofa, with a damp cloth on his forehead. His mother was kneeling by his side, holding his hand, but she was not looking at him. No one was looking at him. They were looking at his father, who stood by the table, rocking up and down on his heels, as if to suggest, in a dignified fashion, he had reason to jump for joy.

". . . covered with dead leaves," he was saying.

Oliver shut his eyes again and listened.

He had not missed much, thanks to his mother's habit of repeating everything his father said, as if she had difficulty in believing it.

"You found it in the old icehouse? The Renoir? What on earth was it doing there?"

Not been burned at all, his father said. Stolen. Cut out of its frame — see the edges? Wrapped in a trash bag, here it is, see it? Hidden in the icehouse —

"But why?" his mother had asked, sounding bewildered. "Why didn't they just take it with them?"

Obvious, surely, wasn't it? his father had said, a trifle irritably. Disturbed in the act. Heard something — dogs, car, how was he supposed to know? Didn't want to be found with the painting on them. Hid it.

"Then the fire . . . ?"

"Dropped a lighted cigarette, no doubt. Careless devils. No respect for property — unless it's portable, what? Then they make off with it. Ha!"

"How terrible," Lady Mallerton had said. "We might have been all burned to death. How wicked people are!"

There were murmurs of agreement.

Oliver lay with his eyes shut and his head spinning, listening to his father in amazement. He knew *he* had hidden the Renoir in the attic, not the icehouse, *he* had cut it out of its frame, *he* had set fire to the gallery. There had been no thieves, only Oliver himself.

He began to wonder if his father were playing a terrible game with him. Perhaps his father had known the truth all the time, and would at any moment say coldly, "Well, my boy, aren't you going to own up like a man? Come on, speak up, it was you, wasn't it? It was my son who was wicked enough to try and destroy Mallerton."

The thought of being so accused and put to shame in front of everyone was terrible, and his hand had trembled in his mother's, attracting her attention. Immediately he had been fussed over, wrapped in a rug, and taken upstairs to bed — and his father had said nothing. Had scarcely glanced at him as he'd left the room.

135

As soon as he was alone in his room, Oliver had jumped out of bed and gone up to the attic. He had climbed on the stool and reached up to the top of the cupboard, expecting to find the painting gone, but to his surprise, his fingers had touched the dusty, sheeted bundle . . .

"And that's where you came in," he said, smiling at Emily. "You took it for your father's painting, but of course, his must be the one they've got, the one downstairs. Do you see now?"

She nodded gloomily.

Oh, she understood, at last. Her father, poor and in debt, must have been all too easily tempted. How often she had heard him boast that he could paint better than Renoir or Rouault, Titian or Turner, or anyone else you cared to mention.

Had he been overheard one night, when he was out with his friends? Or perhaps it was her own resemblance to Sylvia that had first suggested the idea? There were portraits of her, she knew, hanging in the small, back-street London galleries where her father exhibited. Had someone seen one and said, "Why, that could be Sylvia"? And then thought, Yes, yes — why not? *Let* her be Sylvia. Had someone made a careful note of the signature, Benjamin Dodd? The signature! she thought, suddenly hopeful, for there was no law against making a copy. No law, so far as she knew, against faking the copy to look old, as long as . . .

"Is it signed?" she asked.

Oliver nodded. "Renoir, not Dodd," he said, guessing her thoughts. "A. Renoir in the bottom right-hand corner, just like mine."

"Oh."

"It's very good," he said, to comfort her. "You can't tell the difference, honestly. I suppose he copied it from a photograph. She's in our guidebook, you know, and we sell postcards of her. Perhaps he used one of those?"

He must have done, she thought, but then, why use me, too? Unless it was to give that touch of life he always says you can't get from a copy . . . What a lot of trouble he'd been to, having the dress made, finding an old canvas. Was it French? she wondered. Had he been in France the nights he claimed he'd stayed with an old friend whose car had broken down, whose telephone was out of order, whose last bus had been canceled — all those prodigal excuses her mother had obviously disbelieved?

"It must be funny having a father who's a crimi —" Oliver stopped, looked away from her

137

tactfully, and began playing with the ears of his
dog. "I mean, well . . . Did you know?"

"No."

"Bad luck," he said awkwardly, and she realized
he was a long way behind her, still stumbling
about in a mental fog, whereas it was all cold day-
light for her now. Poor Oliver.

"Why did he hide it in our icehouse?" he asked,
after a long pause.

He was nearly there.

"So that it could be found, of course."

"Found?" he repeated stupidly.

"It was meant to be found. Did you think Dad
did it for fun? He took a lot of trouble. Someone
gave him money, someone told him where to hide
it, someone thought up a story to explain it all . . ."
She laughed. "No wonder he wanted everyone to
come! He wanted witnesses!"

"No!" said Oliver sharply. "No, not *my* father!"

She shrugged.

"He wouldn't do anything dishonest! He's a
Mallerton!"

She was unimpressed.

"Besides, why should he?"

"For money," she said. "He can sell it. Dad
couldn't — it never belonged to him. Where could

he say he'd got it from? But your father can. Nobody would question him."

"We don't need money," said Oliver, with insufferable hauteur. "We're rich."

It was then Lady Mallerton chose to come in, bearing milk and cookies on a tarnished silver tray as if it were champagne, and bubbling over with the happiness of someone who has come into a fortune.

"Do you know what a Renoir fetched last week?" she asked them, after she'd shooed the dog off the bed, straightened Oliver's covers, and handed them their milk. The cookies she began idly feeding to the dog. "*Three hundred thousand pounds!* Think of that! Of course, it might've been a *bigger* one, the paper didn't say what size. Oh, my dears, it couldn't have come at a better time! Now I shall be able to sleep at night, instead of lying awake looking at that awful bulge in the ceiling. Oliver, darling, you don't look pleased. Aren't you pleased? I expect there's something you'd like . . ."

"You're not going to sell it?" he asked.

"Of *course,* darling! I'm sorry — I know you were rather fond of it. Do you remember that silly game you used to play? But we need the money.

Father's taking it up to London tomorrow. It has to be remounted or something. He did explain it to me. Not that I understood. Then we must all pray for a *very* rich American, or perhaps an Arab would be better . . ."

When, at long last, she had gone, Emily risked a glance at Oliver. She had half expected he would be near tears, but he met her gaze quite cheerfully. There had been a Mallerton in the eighteenth century, he told her, who had been hanged for highway robbery.

"Oh?" she said, uncertain how to take this.

Another earlier Mallerton had been a privateer, and one had been banished by Henry VII, though he'd forgotten why.

"We've always been an adventurous lot," he said.

She nodded respectfully. If seeing his father's guilt as part of their family tradition comforted him, that was all right with her. She was glad he had found a way to admire his father still.

"You have to hand it to him," he said. "It was a jolly clever idea, wasn't it? No reason why it shouldn't have worked — if your father did his job properly."

"He won't have done!" she said quickly. "He'll have got something wrong, I know he will! He'll be found out! They both will!"

There was no need to get upset, he told her. She wasn't going to cry, was she? It was quite simple. All they had to do was to change the paintings over and nobody'd be any the wiser.

"Nobody," he repeated, his eyes now bright with mischief. "Not my father, nor yours! They'll go ahead, thinking they're selling the fake when all the time it will be the real thing."

Slowly Emily began to smile. She liked the idea, she decided. Serve her father right!

"Every time an expert looks at it closely —" she said.

"They'll shake in their shoes!"

"And if it's X-rayed —"

"My father will pray yours hasn't used an old potato sack for a canvas!" He laughed and added, "How's that for a Sylvia Game? It'll be the best ever!"

"How will you do it?" she asked.

He hesitated. Was it her imagination, or did he look a little embarrassed? He'd worked out a plan while his mother had been talking, he said. His was the most difficult part, but he didn't mind

141

that. It was quite dangerous — he'd have to be careful not to hurt himself. He was going to create a diversion by falling downstairs. Everybody'd come running when he screamed, even his father. All Emily had to do — he seemed apologetic that it was so little — was to slip into the study when his father left it and change over the paintings . . .

"It won't take a minute," he said airily. Then his face suddenly became grave. "Only you mustn't get caught," he warned her. "Father — I don't know what Father would do!"

16

Not far from Sir Robert Mallerton's study door, a large, carved chest was set diagonally across a corner. On top of it was a copper urn holding tall, dusty plumes of pampas grass and the silvery seed-pods of honesty. Behind it was Emily.

I'm going to sneeze, she thought.

She was doubled up on the floor, her head, its conspicuous hair hidden beneath an old navy ski hat of Oliver's, nearly touching the boards. Now, with some difficulty, she extricated one of her arms and brought her hand up to pinch her nose in an attempt to strangle the sneeze. She couldn't — she couldn't — she was going to suffocate . . .

She sneezed.

No door opened. No angry voice demanded

to know who was there. The dust settled softly about her.

Perhaps he was not even in his study.

She wondered how long she would have to wait, with a cramp in every muscle and dust in her nose, and by her side a blue nylon kitbag that had once held Oliver's rolled-up tent and now contained three hundred thousand pounds' worth (possibly) of rolled-up Renoir.

I must've been mad, she thought. Why me? Why couldn't Oliver have done it? He's frightened of his father, that's what! So am I, come to that. And it had been surprisingly difficult, she had found, to resist Oliver's eager, hopeful face. No wonder Kevin had always ended up the one in trouble.

She wished Kevin were here now. He would not be frightened. He would not be crouching down, with a pain in his belly and his back aching as if every vertebra were a rotten tooth. She *had* to move! Slowly, carefully, she straightened up and gazed through the pampas grass toward the study door.

It opened.

She made no attempt to duck down again behind the chest. Like a frightened rabbit, she froze, her dark clothes invisible against the paneled walls behind her, her face pale as the pampas grass through which she stared.

The man who came striding out was as red as a fox. Red hair, red face, short, stiff red moustache — even his hands were red. There was nothing else foxlike about him, however. His chin was not pointed but full and fleshy. He was tall, with great shoulders and a thick neck, and hot brown eyes. A bad-tempered bull of a man.

He did not glance her way, but walked briskly down the passage and out of sight.

Now her cramped corner seemed warm and safe, and the short stretch of polished floor between her and the study door as uninviting as a river full of crocodiles. Come on, Emily, she told herself. The pampas grass shook as she moved. Her rubber soles squeaked. Now she was in the study, the door shut behind her and her heart still knocking as if it had been left outside and wanted desperately to come in.

Calm down. Breathe in. Breathe out. There's no one in the study but you. It won't take a minute . . .

If only her fingers were not shaking so much. She could not loosen the string of the kitbag. Careful, there's a knot . . . There, that's done it! The string ran smoothly through the eyelets, the bag opened, and she drew out the Renoir. Then she heard the footsteps.

He was coming back!

She must hide! Where? The heavy steps were nearly at the door. Quick! Hide! Don't try to face it out. People have been murdered for pennies, let alone a Renoir. Where? Behind that desk? Too far. Behind the chair —

As she crouched down, the brass handle began to turn.

Then in the distance, someone screamed. There was a muffled thumping, and someone screamed again, three times. True to his word, Oliver had fallen downstairs.

The handle, abruptly released, spun back. There was the sound of a key turning in the lock. Then footsteps, half running, thundered down the passage. She was locked in.

She was terribly frightened. Then she remembered the windows and the open garden beyond. It was all right. She was not trapped. Now she moved quickly. There was a loose roll of canvas on the table by the window. Her father's painting? Better check. Yes, a brief glimpse of the changeling face and red-gold hair before she let the canvas roll up again.

A clock struck harshly behind her, making her jump. Half-past twelve. Nearly lunchtime. Lunch? Sir Robert, may I present Emily Dodd, the faker's daughter. . . . No. No lunch for Emily. A quick escape through the window — *it wouldn't open!*

They were casement windows with small square panes. None of them would open. The latches turned, the windows gave a little and then stopped, held at the bottom by some sort of metal fastening with a small round hole. Must be for some sort of key. Where would they keep it? In this jug? No, only dust and a burned match. Behind the clock? No. In the desk drawers? Pencils, paper clips . . . what was this? A shining metal rod with a round handle, like a sardine-can opener. If only her fingers wouldn't tremble so . . .

It fit.

She snatched up the roll of canvas and thrust it into the kitbag, leaving the other one in its place. She had the window open when she heard someone coming. She was astride the sill when the door opened. Then she was running madly, the

147

kitbag bumping against her side, over the gravel, onto the grass, leaping the miniature hedges that patterned the lawn, the furious voice bellowing out behind her, "Stop! Stop, thief! Head him off, Rogers, you old fool!"

In front of her now, an old man with a surprised, weather-beaten face and faded blue eyes — he was holding a garden fork in his hands. She dodged away. A quick glance over her shoulder showed her Sir Robert, pushing himself with some difficulty through the narrow window. Now there were voices on her left. Oh God, they'd catch her!

She turned again, raced across the drive into the shelter of some shrubs, down a path, looking desperately for somewhere to hide. Here was the gate to the Maze! Without stopping to think, she climbed into the false security of the tall, dark, enclosing hedges. As she ran out of sight down a narrow leafy corridor, she heard Sir Robert behind her, shouting.

"There he goes!"

And another man's voice cried, "Tally-ho!" and laughed.

More voices. "We've got 'im now. 'E's trapped!"

"No, don't follow him in! Spread out. You two go round that way. Rogers, you go that!"

"Fetch the ladder! You'll spot 'im then!"

"Good idea. Off you go, Burton."

"Let the dogs loose!"

Who were all these people? Where had they sprung from? Servants of Mallerton? Friends? Visitors? The Maze, which had seemed so huge and endless, appeared to have shrunk. Voices came clearly from all sides. She was surrounded.

As she crouched in a blind alley, trembling, she heard through the leaves a woman's voice, close at hand, say, "I've brought your gun, Sir Robert."

Gun! Were they going to *shoot* her? What did they think she was, a rabbit? What kind of people were these, to hunt a fellow creature with such enjoyment?

Now Sir Robert spoke; his voice, sounding very near, was loud, authoritative, and satisfied.

"Can you hear me? We have you surrounded. And I have a gun. Better give yourself up quietly, boy."

Boy? thought Emily, confused for a moment into thinking there was another child in the Maze. Then she remembered her long hair was hidden beneath a cap. She tiptoed back the way she had come and chose another path, walking softly, her eyes fixed to the base of the hedges.

There was wire netting over a gap here. She knelt down and peered through, fearing to see another concrete path, another high hedge, but there was only grass. Empty grass. She listened. There were voices, but none near at hand. Carefully, trying to make as little noise as possible, she untangled the netting from the leaves and twigs and pulled it away from the hedge.

She peered through. She could still see only grass and some trees some distance away, but the hedge was thick and restricted her vision. Taking a deep breath, she began forcing her way through the gap, shutting her eyes against the leaves and twigs that brushed her face.

When she opened her eyes again, she saw a pair of muddy boots standing in the grass in front of her.

The old man was looking down at her. He still had his garden fork. With his large, knotted hands on the handle, he was leaning on it, while his pale, watery eyes regarded her without expression. Then, after glancing quickly to the right and to the left, he jerked his head toward the grove behind him.

"Git off, then, ye poor little fox," he said.

Emily, with a startled, joyous smile of gratitude,

was on her feet and running silently away from the Maze and into the cover of the trees.

The gardener watched her out of sight; then, hearing Sir Robert shouting from the other side of the Maze, gave a small, crooked smile.

"Call me an old fool, would 'e?" he muttered.

17

It was already getting dark as the bus came to the outskirts of Swanham Bay. Though it was only half-past five, the gray day was heavy with the coming night.

Emily, sitting slumped in her seat, saw with quiet joy the lights springing up in the small, solid houses, the glitter of a passing sweet-shop window, and the smooth roads, edged with neat yellow lines instead of stinking ditches full of brambles and barbed wire. The little town, done up in its yellow ribbons and sparkling lights like a Christmas parcel, seemed beautiful to her.

She had had enough of the country. Its mud still clung to her shoes, its filthy water still oozed between the toes of her blistered feet, its thorns still held shreds of her skin and tatters of her clothing.

Never had she run so far nor so fast as she had run from Mallerton. Through the grove, past the lake, through the plantation of firs, with the shouting and the yapping of dogs dying away behind her, until at last, breathless, her sides aching, her heels in ribbons, she came to the high wall and, following this around, found a tree leaning against it, its branches low enough to reach.

On the other side, a soft bed of stinging nettles awaited her, and a muddy cart track with a plowed field beyond. No signpost. No bus stop. No café. Just the country, stretching out drearily in all directions, and no telling which way to go.

Now, four weary hours later, she sat in the bus, wet, exhausted, and starving. I shall be ill again, she thought comfortably. I shall be put in a warm bed and fed hot chicken soup and grapes and chocolate. And people will say, "Poor Emily."

The bus stopped and she got off, holding the kitbag carefully, and hobbled painfully along the pavement, waiting for a chance to cross the road. A pack of motorcyclists roared by, shouting something to a group of youths who sat or leaned idly on the sea wall.

"And the same to you, you frigging lubbers!" one shouted back.

He was tall and thin and had a crest of green hair running along the top of his head. A punk. Sitting against the dying light of the sky, he looked like a strange prehistoric bird. He watched the riders out of sight and then jumped down from the wall and said, in a sour, restless voice, "We sitting 'ere all night, then?"

His discontented eyes caught sight of Emily.

" 'Oo you staring at, baby? 'Ow come your mum lets you out alone? Ben't she warned you about the bad boys?"

Oh, no! This is too much, thought Emily. She gave a careful, propitiating smile and, seeing no gap in the home-going traffic, edged nervously away down the pavement.

Behind her she could hear the soft thud of rubber-soled feet as the boys jumped off the wall, and then she was surrounded by a jostling, jeering crowd. One snatched the cap off her head, and they cheered and shrieked as her long hair tumbled down.

"Jist look at 'er flaming 'air!"

"Hey, Gingernut, can I 'ave a bite?"

"Oo, she's going to cry! Give 'er back 'er 'at!"

"Catch!"

But the hat was thrown high above her head to

a boy behind her, who laughed and threw it to another youth. Let them keep it! She didn't care! It wasn't hers.

But now she felt someone tugging at the strings of the kitbag and snatched it away in alarm.

"Let go! Leave me alone!"

"Jist want to carry it for you, baby. Doing the polite, that's all. Keep your 'air on. What you got in there, anyway? Been up to something, 'ave you? Come on, let's 'ave a look."

"Yeah, come on! Let's see."

"Leave me alone or I'll scream!" she said desperately, and stepped back, only to bump into someone behind her.

"Mind my toes, clumsy!"

It was Kevin. In the dusk, with his black leather jacket and his long black hair and his earring glittering in the lamplight, he looked different. Fiercer. She wasn't certain whose side he was on. But he said easily, with a friendly smile, "Lay off, mates. This is my little bird. I got to take her home to her tea or my mum will have the skin off me."

The youths looked at him. He seemed small beside them; they were all much older and taller. One or two said, amiably enough, " 'Ullo, Kev." The others just looked.

"She your chick, then?" one of them asked.

"My cousin," said Kevin, with no hesitation.

"Oh."

"We was only horsing around," said one.

"She can 'ave 'er 'at back, if she says 'please,'" said another.

"Fair enough," said Kevin, and turned to Emily, who said "Please" obediently, having no false pride. A youth handed her the hat and grinned. She smiled back. They were only boys. No need to be frightened. They parted to let her and Kevin through — but the way was suddenly blocked by a tall figure. It was the green-crested punk.

"I wanna see what she got in that there bag fust," he said aggressively.

"Leave her be," said Kevin.

There was a pause. The youths looked from Kevin to the punk and drew back a little, making a ring round them. Someone giggled. A hand caught Emily and tried to drag her away from Kevin's side, but she shook it off. A voice said, "Let 'im 'ave it, Sid! Do 'im!"

"It's only a painting!" cried Emily quickly. "One of my dad's. He's an artist!"

"Whad'ja take me for?" the punk said angrily. "A thick-'ead? You couldn't get no picture in there!" She had offended him. He thought she was making a game of him in front of his gang; now she was not going to get away before he had humbled her.

"It's rolled up! It's on canvas!" she said desperately.

"Show it."

"Yeah, show it!" said a pale, pretty youth with pink hair.

"Show it! Show it!" joined in the other boys, closing in.

Her father's fake — how could she? They were local boys. They might well have been to Mallerton House.

"Why should I?" she said, backing nervously away.

Hands struck her from behind, pushed, and now she was staggering forward into the arms of the green-crested punk.

"Can't leave me alone, can you, baby?" he crowed, holding her tightly round the waist, bending his bird's face as if to peck at her. His breath stank of stale tobacco. She kicked him on the shin and he swore, letting her go. Before he had time to grab her again, Kevin was in the way. He was still smiling, but his dark eyes were wary.

"Oh, let her go, Sid," he said. "She's only small. Not worth bothering about —"

"Throw 'er back in the sea!" suggested one, and they all laughed. Sid grabbed Kevin by the ear and twisted it. Kevin yelped in pain.

"What 'ave we 'ere?" said the punk. "What's this between me fingers?" He transferred his grip to Kevin's hair and jerked back his head. Kevin struggled in vain, but two youths held his arms. The earring, now decorated by a ruby of blood, gleamed in the streetlight. "Gold is it? Real gold, eh?" Sid's small eyes were greedy. "Don't suit 'im, do it?" he said to his followers. Some tittered. Others looked uneasy. "You going to 'and it over, or am I going to 'ave to tear your ear off?"

Kevin's gold earring that he wore so proudly, in memory of the handsome gypsy who might have been his father . . .

"Don't!" Emily cried. "Look, I'll show it to you!" She dragged the canvas out of the bag. "Look!" she said, but they ignored her. They were enjoying themselves, watching Kevin with avid interest.

"Don't hurt me," he mumbled, sounding frightened. "You can have it. I'll take it out. Let go of my hands —" They did. Kevin promptly punched the crested punk in the stomach.

It was no fair fight. Kevin did not stand a chance. Emily saw him go down under a pile of youths. "Do 'im!" someone was shouting gleefully. "Do 'im over proper!"

Emily screamed. Shrill and high, the sound rang out, drowning the noise of traffic and the laughter of the boys, startling the seagulls, who sent back harsh echoing cries, surprising even herself. She had no idea she could make so much noise. The youths stopped and looked uneasily over their shoulders. "Put a sock in it," one muttered. "You'll 'ave the pigs onto us. We wasn't doing nothing!" " 'e ben't 'urt," said another, pulling Kevin roughly to his feet, but keeping hold of his arm and looking toward his leader as if for instructions. Sid was scowling. Emily could see the indecision on his face. He glanced toward Emily, and the sight of her seemed to aggravate him. Then his eye fell to the roll of canvas in her hand.

"Look," she said with a timid smile, unrolling the canvas as far as she could. "It's a portrait of me."

They all stared at it. She waited, trembling, for a

voice to say, "That's not hers! That's from Mallerton. I seen it there," but it did not come.

"I'll be beggared!" said Sid. "She were telling the frigging truth! Jest look at that!" The violence drained from him suddenly; perhaps he was glad of a chance to back down without losing face. "Not bad, eh?" he said.

Immediately their mood changed. They all admired it. Thought it a smashing likeness. Said her dad must be a blooming genius. Laughing and shoving, they offered each other as models. Kevin, brushing the dust off his leather jacket, did not laugh. Silently he stared at the painting, then at Emily, then at the painting again.

Only when they were alone, walking back to the hotel together, did he open his mouth.

"You're *mad!*" he said in a fierce whisper, looking uneasily over his shoulder. "What've you been and done, you little fool? That's the Ren — Renoyer you got there, worth hundreds and thousands of pounds! And you go showing it to the biggest snitch in Dorset!" Then, after a moment's thought, he added comfortingly, "Still, don't suppose he'd know what he was looking at. He ben't got no eye for nothing above a transistor."

160

18

"A' course, if you don't trust me," said Kevin.

Emily had told him it was not the Renoir. He had not believed her. She had told him it was only a copy. He said she was a liar. They walked side by side down the darkening street. A cold, salty wind blew off the sea, and it was beginning to rain.

"What's up with your feet?" asked Kevin, seeing her limp.

"Blisters."

"Serve you right," he said, still offended.

"It's not my secret! I'd tell you if I could, honest! Only — I gave my hand of honor —"

"Ah!" He looked at her sharply. "Your hand, was it? Only one person as I ever heard call it that. Very free with his hands of honor, is Master Oliver! Thing is — can you trust him?"

She began to cry. Once started, there seemed no good reason to stop. Compared to the rain, her tears were warm and comforting. She hid her face in her handkerchief and felt she was shutting out the whole dingy, dishonorable world.

"Oh, put a sock in it!" said Kevin, when his attempts to comfort her had failed. "Stop your sniveling, will you! We're back. D'you want your dad to see you like this?"

She did.

She was very content to be comforted and cosseted, be wrapped in her father's arms and to hear from their shelter Mrs. Dewy exclaiming in concern over the state of her feet.

"Oh, the poor little pet! Like a drowned rabbit, she is! Now, don't worry over the mud on the carpet, 'twill come off easy. Just you put her in a hot bath and bed afore she catches her death."

Over her father's shoulder, as he carried her upstairs, Emily caught sight of Kevin, staring after her with the baffled expression of a cat who'd lost his favorite mouse; and she could not resist giving a small, triumphant smile.

"Ah, she's feeling better already," said Mrs. Dewy. Kevin said nothing. He was now looking dejected.

"Oh!" said Emily, remembering that he'd helped

her and she had not even thanked him, but before she had time to say more, her father had carried her, rather clumsily, round the bend in the stairs.

"What's the matter, Em? Did I hurt you?" he said, and she wanted to say yes, he had hurt her very badly indeed. Instead she buried her face in his shoulder and said nothing.

Kevin watched Emily out of sight. He was feeling angry. He hated secrets from which he was excluded. Little prig, giving herself airs with her hand of honor! He hoped her bathwater was too hot and made her blisters burn! He hoped she got arrested for stealing the Renoir and put in jail!

"Come and have your tea, Kevin," said his mother, but he said he had an important telephone call to make first.

The hotel office was empty. He dialed the number and waited, looking at an old poster advertising the attractions at Mallerton House. Great hall, linenfold-paneled dining room, famous paintings . . . He sneered.

The voice that answered was new to him, for which he was thankful. There were some there that wouldn't be pleased to hear him again.

"Can I speak to Oliver?" he said. "Tell him it's — an old friend."

"Can I have your name, please."

"A friend. Just tell him a friend." Was it true any longer? he wondered.

There was a pause, then the voice said doubtfully, "Will you hold on, please."

Why did I do that? thought Kevin. Surely he'd not refuse to speak to me.

Now Oliver's voice came, breathless as if he'd been running. Slightly nervous.

"This is Oliver Mallerton. Who's that, please?"

"Me. Kevin."

"Kevin! You old idiot, why didn't you give your name? I thought . . . How are you?"

"Fine."

"How's — how's your mother?"

"Fine. And yours?"

"Fine."

There was a pause, in which he could hear Oliver breathing quickly.

"Ben't you going to ask about Emily?" he said, making his voice heavy with significance, although of what he only had a confused idea.

"Emily — why, did she — did she say anything?"

"What do *you* think, mate?" Heavy sarcasm.

"You mean, she told you!"

Kevin shrugged; then, realizing this was wasted on the telephone, said, "Ever known a bird what didn't sing?"

Oliver swore. He had trusted her, he said bitterly. Kevin, knowing his trick had worked, felt no elation, merely a sour guilt.

"You don't want to trust nobody," he said sadly.

It was easy now. With only a little prompting, the whole tale came tumbling out, somewhat mixed up but clear enough for anyone with two good ears and a quick brain between them. He relaxed. Whatever he had suspected, it had been worse than this. Faking a picture? That wasn't so bad, he thought with relief. Not like stealing one. As Oliver talked, the constraint that had come between them seemed to melt away. Listening to his friend's quick, excited voice, Kevin could have been back by the schoolroom fire, or sitting high in the branches of the apple tree, while Oliver planned their next mischief. He made it sound like the Sylvia Game.

"I wish I'd been there," he said wistfully.

"I wish you had! Do you know what that girl did? She climbed out of the study window, with Father and Mardie and Tim Brent, oh, and everybody in hot pursuit! Damned idiot! Why couldn't she have just hidden or something?"

Nowhere much to hide, thought Kevin, remembering the study. She's brave enough, is Titch, for all her tears. She'd not have run 'less she had to.

"She bolted into the Maze and I thought they had her cornered," went on Oliver. "I nearly died! I went cold all over. But she got out somehow. And then they set the dogs after her . . ."

Poor Emily, with those great dogs baying at her heels. No wonder she'd run through bogs and briars. He saw her like a rocket on Guy Fawkes night, shooting through the dark with her bright hair streaming behind her.

"How did she get away?" he asked.

"Jasper saved her," Oliver said proudly. "He started a fight with Tavin, and all the other dogs joined in. Father was furious! I've had to hide Jasper in the old barn or he'd have him shot."

That bleeding man, thought Kevin, with sudden, bitter anger. Someone ought to stand up to him! Why doesn't Oliver tell him to go to hell? I would, surely. Still, I ben't his son. And he always had a soft spot for me — I dunno why, but I could tell, somehow. A' course, I was only a servant's son, but sometimes, sometimes he'd look from Oliver to me, almost as if he wished 'twas the other way round and I was his boy. No, that's bad! Poor Oliver! Ben't his fault he's delicate. Ben't my virtue I'm tough, neither. Just the way it fell.

"You know, they thought she was a boy," Oliver was saying now. "Wasn't that lucky? She was wearing a ski hat — *mine,* I hope she hasn't lost it. They never connected 'him' with Emily. They didn't even remember her till lunch. Then Mother — you know what she's like with names — said, 'Where's little Annabel?' and Mardie said, 'I thought she was called Emily.' And I said, just to confuse them further, 'No, it's Sylvia and she was cross because she couldn't ride, so she went home in a huff.' They all started talking about the bad manners of modern youth and that kept them busy till the end of the meal. Wasn't I clever?"

Kevin agreed.

"So'm I clever," he said. "I tricked you, Ollie. She didn't give you away. She never said nothing. Her hand of honor's lily-white, least, where it ben't covered with scratches. You didn't send her home in good condition, you know. She's a very poor, tattered little sparrow now."

When he put the receiver down, he sat shaking his head. Who'd have thought it of Sir Robert, who'd lectured them many a time on the standards of behavior he expected, standing stiff and upright in his study, tapping the punishing cane against his leg? Still, was it so surprising, at that? See him on the hunting field, trampling over other people's crops and hedges, without a care but for what he was after! See him wave the bloody tail above his head, without a thought for the little fox what might've wanted to keep it! Then you'd have knowed he'd stop at little to save Mallerton, and a way of life that was better gone.

It won't be one picture, neither, thought Kevin, frowning. Not with him thinking he's got away with it, and Oliver ben't planning to tell him different. He'll think he's found his ladder to fortune, but that's the head of the snake he's put his foot on. Someone ought to tell him afore he goes sliding down.

Not me! What do I care? I ben't his son, after all. None of my business. But he sat frowning at the telephone for some time, as if hoping someone would ring him and tell him what to do.

19

Emily lay in bed. She was warm now, and clean and comfortable, but she could not sleep. In the long drawer at the bottom of the wardrobe, the painting, safe in its kitbag, was hidden beneath her spare nightgown. She had meant to confront her father with it. Many times, when stumbling through ditch and bramble, she had thought with fierce pleasure of throwing the fake in her father's face. She had not done so. The face had been so kind and concerned that the angry words had dissolved on her tongue like sherbet. She had said nothing. I'm a fool, she thought crossly.

She thumped her pillow and turned over. On her bedside table, in the dim light from the window, she saw a pale oblong. Kevin's card. She had not seen him again. Her father had insisted that she go straight to bed and had brought up her supper tray himself, with the card on it.

It was a sheet of drawing paper, folded in half. On the front was the picture of a monkey with its hands over its mouth and a yellow ring in one ear. Inside was written: "Hope you are better. Don't worry about nothing. Secrets a Specialty of the House. Kevin."

"What's all this about secrets?" her father had said.

As she had hesitated, seeing an opening, he had gone on to say, "Never mind. I shouldn't have asked, should I? You keep your little secrets," in such an indulgent, patronizing way that she had shut her mouth with a snap.

She sighed and turned over again. Now she could see the dark bulk of the wardrobe and the faint gleam of the brass handles on the drawer in which the painting was hidden. "Get rid of it," Oliver had said.

Get rid of it. She saw herself throwing it in the sea. She saw the canvas slowly unfurling. Once more a pale girl gazed up through the green water: Sylvia drowned again. No! The fire in the hotel lounge . . . burn it . . . She saw flames springing up like bright hair around a child's face, blisters appearing on the white cheeks: Sylvia burning. "No," muttered Emily, turning restlessly in her bed.

She was lying in moonlight! False squares patterned her bed and the floor. All else was dark. There had been a noise. Now it came again, a small sound . . . tap, tap, tap.

Her glance flew to the window, but she saw only the white moon and a silver rooftop against the black sky.

Tap, tap, tap.

It was coming from the drawer at the bottom of the wardrobe, and as she watched, the drawer began slowly to open. From the dark slit, two eyes glittered like stars. A pale hand thrust out, with thin green weeds like ribbons interlacing the fingers. Something dropped from it onto the floor, and a small brown frog went leaping away under the bed.

Someone was screaming! Someone was sitting up in bed and screaming! Why didn't they do something? Why didn't they let poor Sylvia out of the drawer?

The light was switched on and her father stood there in his pajamas.

"What is it? What's the matter? What's happened?"

"It's Sylvia! It's Sylvia! She's in that drawer! Look!"

"Oh, poor Emmie, it's only a nightmare. Lord, what a shriek! I thought the hotel was on fire."

"Don't let her burn! Let her out! She wants to get out!"

"Emily! Emily, wake up! There's nothing there. Look, I'll show you."

The last shreds of nightmare cleared from her head and she saw, before he opened it, that the drawer was shut tight.

"Now what have we here? One nightie," her father said, taking it out of the drawer and holding it up, showing her first one side and then the other, like a conjurer proving there was no deception. "Nothing inside. And an old kitbag — let me see, can we have a monster in here, frightening my poor little daughter?" He smiled at her and began loosening the string. Emily made no attempt to stop him. It was fate, she thought; the truth *wanted* to come out. She hadn't told. Now her father had the bag open and was looking inside. His face changed. He gave her a sharp glance, drew out the canvas, and unrolled it.

"Oh, my God!" he said.

He turned the painting to the light and studied

it intently. There was no sign of guilt on his face, only intense concentration. He held it at first at arm's length, then close to his face. Then he laid it on the floor, as gently as if the girl in the white dress were sleeping and he did not want to wake her. He weighted it down at the corners with enormous care, using her slippers and his own; then crouched down before it, staring.

"It's good, damn him," he said at last. "It's far better than mine."

She watched him in bewilderment. The scene was so different from any she had imagined, scenes in which she had accused angrily and he had broken down and confessed. When at last he remembered her, he turned abruptly and said, "Where the devil did you get hold of this?"

"I can't tell you. It's a secret."

He bit his lip.

"Now, Emily," he said, coming to sit by her bed, taking her hands in his, "don't be silly. This is serious. You have to tell me. Don't be frightened. I won't be angry."

She shook her head stubbornly.

"Give me patience," he muttered. "Emily, this isn't a game. Good heavens, child, do you know what you've got there?"

"Yes!" she shouted. "Your bloody fake, that's what!"

That silenced him. He dropped her hands and stared at her. His face was quite blank, like a mask. He looked again at the painting and then made an odd sound in his throat, like a strangled laugh.

"The dress!" he said. "You recognized the dress and thought . . . Emily, my poor girl, this isn't a fake —"

He was trying to bluff it out. He did not trust her. Bitterly hurt, she shouted, "Don't lie! Don't lie to me!"

"Hush! Not so loud! Do you want to wake the whole hotel?" He crossed quickly to the door and bolted it, then came slowly back to her. "Look, Emily, it's true I made a copy of the Renoir —"

"A copy!" she interrupted, furious tears coming into her eyes. She blinked them away. "Why did you fake it to look old, then? Why did you lock the studio door? Why did you go to France?"

"To France?" he said in astonishment. "In heaven's name, Emily, what's France got to do with it? I've never been to France."

"Don't lie, Dad. It's no good. I know everything."

"Do you, indeed? I wish I did," he said dryly.

174

"Perhaps you wouldn't mind putting me in the picture, Emily. Tell me —"

"I can't! I won't! I gave my hand of honor," she said, and then added bitterly, "Honor, I don't suppose that means anything to *you!*"

He did not flush. Instead, a look of such intense exasperation came into his face that she shrank back against the pillows. When he lifted his hand, she flinched.

"Emily!" he said in surprise. "You're not frightened of me, are you?"

She did not answer.

"I wasn't going to hit you! I've never hit you, have I?"

She shook her head and looked away from him, down at her hands. She could feel him watching her.

"All right, Emily," he said at last. "If you've given your word of honor, you must keep it, I suppose." There was now no trace of the condescension with which he had mentioned her "little secrets." For the first time, he spoke to her as if she were a person in her own right, not just a child to be patted on the head and dismissed with a joking word. "I know you think I break my

175

promises, but that's not fair. I'm very careful *never* to make a definite promise. 'Maybe' and 'we'll see' aren't the same thing at all, Emily. You seem to be suffering under a misapprehension. Several misapprehensions, in fact. Now listen. I didn't fake my painting to look old — no, don't interrupt! It's true I used an old canvas. I often do, as you ought to know, but it was a perfectly straightforward copy, with my own name at the bottom as the copyist."

"Dad, look at it!" she said. "Look at the cracks! Look at the signature!"

"Emily, this is the original," he said gently. "God knows where you got it from. He told me it had been destroyed in the fire."

She stared at him.

"It isn't! It can't be!" she said. "It's yours!"

"Do you think I don't know my own work? I'm not blind. This is a Renoir. Unmistakable." He looked down at the painting and shook his head wonderingly. "I never thought I'd hold one in my hands."

Emily was desperately trying to remember . . . The two rolls of canvas on the table, her father's on the left, the Renoir on the right. She was not a fool; she had realized the danger of muddling them up and had made a special note of it. She had been looking for the key to the window, in the jug, behind the clock, then the table drawer, where she had found it . . . Opened the window, grabbed the painting on the left, the *left,* she was sure of it, turned and . . . Oh! She was on the wrong side of the table! The other side! Everything was back to front.

She looked wildly at the painting on the floor and saw at one corner, half hidden by the slipper that held it down, a jagged tear. "I cut it out of its frame," Oliver had said. "It was quite easy. I only jagged it a little at one corner."

"It's the wrong one!" she cried. "Dad, I've taken the wrong one! What are we going to do?"

"We'll have to take it back," he said.

20

They talked long into the night. Emily, tired and bewildered, felt like a piece of paper on which people were printing different pictures, one after another, until the colors blurred. Her father was explaining everything, sweeping the old suspicions from her head as if they were cobwebs. He had not been to France, he told her, but to Tom Crabbe's, just as he had said. He couldn't imagine why she should doubt it —

"Mum didn't believe you," said Emily.

"What do you mean? Of course she believed me. What on earth gave you that idea?"

Emily could not remember. It was nothing her mother had actually *said*, but . . .

"She was cross," she mumbled.

"Cross? Was she?" He sounded surprised.

"Well, she's never taken to old Tom, but . . . Oh, you mean the time I missed the last bus and couldn't let her know —"

"Why not?"

"Because our telephone was cut off," he said shortly. He had forgotten, as usual, to pay the bill. Was that why he had looked guilty? Only *that?*

And the locked studio door, he went on, didn't she remember? A tube of Chinese vermilion had been knocked off his worktable and trodden on, leaving small, expensive footprints all over the floor.

"Do you know how much Chinese vermilion costs?" he asked now. "Fifteen pounds a tube!"

As for the dress, he had bought it for her because, when he'd been given the color transparency of the Renoir to work from, he'd thought how pretty she would look in such a dress. (He was always buying her presents, and much thanks he got for it!)

"Besides, it gave me the chance to make a few practice sketches," he added with cheerful innocence. "You know I always prefer working from a model. I wanted to get the feel of Renoir's style. I even got you to stand in the same pose, don't you remember?"

She was speechless.

"Mrs. Adkins made it for me," he went on. "Really, Emily, would I choose such a near neighbor to do it if I were involved in something criminal? Or do you suspect poor Mrs. Adkins of being in the plot?"

She shook her head. Mrs. Adkins was an old lady who, even on a summer day, wore a tweed coat with bulging pockets, from which she would take a crumpled bag of aniseed balls whenever she met Tim or Emily. They did not like them but could not tell her so, as she was deaf and had a hearing aid that whistled, making Tim laugh.

Emily felt completely confused. Had she built up a tower of suspicion out of nothing but a few straws? A guilty look, a locked door, a feeling that something was being kept from her, a secret from which she was shut out . . . She remembered conversations that broke off when she entered the room, angry voices that woke her in the night ("It's nothing, Emmie. Of course we weren't having a row! Go back to sleep"). Had it only been about money? Was that all?

"I don't know," she said helplessly. "I don't know who to believe anymore."

He bit his lip and looked at her with compassion.

"My poor girl, it was the bailiffs, wasn't it? You never trusted me after that, and who can blame you? God knows, I felt terrible about it, Rose crying and you children looking as if the end of the world had come. Our poor furniture, that we'd saved so hard for and mended and patched so often, being carried away by strangers . . . And I had to try and joke about it — well, it's my way, but it didn't help, did it? No wonder you looked at me as if I were a fool. What can I say now? I *am* telling the truth, but I don't know how to convince you of it. Except . . . Emily, you said you'd taken the wrong painting. Did you see the other one? Mine?"

"Yes."

"Come now, did it look old? Did it have crackleture?" he said, smiling.

"Yes," she said.

"What!"

"Honest, Dad, it looked exactly the same, cracks and all."

"Well, I'll be damned! Are you *sure?*"

She nodded. "Positive."

He stared at her.

"Emily, that painting was in mint condition when I handed it over in London —"

"In London?" she interrupted, surprised.

"Yes — oh, I see. You thought we came down here so that I could . . . No, no, I delivered it over a month ago. But, well, when the doctor said you needed a change of air, I thought, why not? I wanted to see how my painting looked in an ancestral gallery, among the Old Masters," he confessed childishly. "Not that there were any, as it turned out, a worthless bunch. I suppose he'd sold all the good ones. And my painting wasn't even there. Now you say the paint has *cracked* . . . I can't understand it. Unless there's another copy. Did you see the signature?"

She shook her head. "I only unrolled it a little."

"Unrolled it? Wasn't it on a stretcher?"

"No. It was just like this one. Cut out. And — someone — told me it was signed Renoir. Just A. Renoir. Nothing else."

"Good God!" he said. He sat silently for a long time, frowning, while Emily watched him. She wished she could see inside his head.

"How did you meet Sir Robert?" she asked.

"Bit of luck, that, or so I thought at the time. He saw that portrait of you in the window of Greenip's gallery last year and was very struck by the resemblance. "Extraordinary," he kept saying. "Could be the same girl, what?" I suppose you do look alike to the undiscerning eye. He told me the Renoir had been destroyed in a fire some time ago, and he wanted a copy to hang in its place. Offered me a hundred for expenses and three thousand when I handed the painting over. *Three thousand!* More than double what I get for my original work! I took him for a fool. Now I'm beginning to wonder what he's taken me for ... Surely he couldn't imagine ... He couldn't be that stupid! I was bound to find out. Unless he had a private buyer lined up? No questions asked. I wonder ... no, it doesn't make sense! If he had the original all the time —"

"He didn't," said Emily. "He thinks it was burnt." Her father looked at her in surprise, and she added, her voice rising, "Someone hid it! I can't tell you any more. Please don't ask me! *Please!*"

"All right, darling," he said gently. He gazed absently round the room and his eye fell on Kevin's card. He sat staring at it thoughtfully.

Emily wanted to say it wasn't Kevin, but she could hardly deny what her father had not yet suggested. He might be thinking of something else altogether. He might not be thinking at all. He looked tired.

She wanted so much to believe him. She hated the anxious, doubting person she had become since the bailiffs had carried off their home and half her childhood. "You're an old miser!" Tim had complained. "You never give me anything anymore." She thought of the twenty pounds she had in her bank account, the book hidden in a suitcase on top of her wardrobe, and it no longer gave her any pleasure. It could not buy back what she had lost. She wanted to be a small girl again, flinging her arms around her father's neck and saying she loved him. But she could not. Her arms remained stiffly by her sides as if she were bound in a cocoon from which she could not break out; and her voice, when she spoke, sounded thin and sharp.

"Why didn't you tell us, then? If it was all so innocent, why make a secret of it?"

For the first time, the shifty, guilty look she remembered so well came back into his face.

"I don't know if I can make you understand," he said, and sighed.

She waited.

"I know you think I'm selfish," he said at last. "I suppose I am. God knows, I often feel guilty . . . Your mother works so hard and doesn't get much fun out of life, poor darling. You children have to go without things — holidays, color telly, radios, all these essentials of modern life! And all I do is paint. It's all I've ever wanted to do. I don't care how poor we are. I don't care if my clothes are in holes or the curtains have shrunk or the rugs are threadbare. In my defense, I told your mother this before we were married. I told her we'd probably always be poor. I told her I was hopeless with money. She said she didn't mind. She said she'd look after the money, she'd look after everything . . . But it's different when one has children. We couldn't ask you how you felt about it, not before you were born, and then it was too late. I know she worried. Not that she ever complained — at least, not to me." He looked anxiously at Emily. "Has she . . . ?"

"No," said Emily quickly, for he suddenly looked old and tired. "She never complains. In fact, she shuts me up . . ." She stopped.

"When *you* complain," her father finished for her. "I can't blame you. You know, sometimes I wake up in the night and think — supposing I'm wrong? Supposing I'm not as good as I think I am? I get up and go into the studio to reassure myself. And there on the wall is the portrait I did of your mother before we were married. So pretty and so young — it could almost be a portrait of you! I stand there thinking, What have I done to her? What have I done to them all? And for what? Supposing I'm no good, no bloody good at all . . ."

"You are good, Dad! Everyone at school says you're clever!"

He smiled at that.

"Oh well, in the morning, it all looks different," he said. "The sun shines and I'm a genius again! You wanted to know why I made a secret of what I was doing? Well, I'll tell you. It was because I was afraid if you found out how much I was getting for the copy, you'd all nag at me to go on doing them. And I didn't want to. I'm not a copyist. I want to do my own work. So much for my moods of remorse, eh?"

She believed him at last! She believed him completely. It might seem an absurd reason to others, but for her it wore a family face. Once she'd been chosen to sing in the school concert and she had not told them just because she had been afraid they'd nag at her to wear the silly white dress. And

Tim! Tim, when he had been given his first school report to take home with him, had hidden it, unopened, under his mattress, in case it was bad. Even their mother, when she had scorched Dad's favorite shirt, had stuffed it quickly into her ragbag, hoping he would not miss it until she could afford another like it.

Her father might not be the shining knight she had thought him when she was small, but she did not care. He was not a criminal, either. He was just . . . like the rest of them, one of the family, full of small faults and overlarge dreams.

"First thing tomorrow I'll take this up to Mallerton House," he said. He began rolling the painting up. "I shan't feel easy until it's back in the right hands. Don't worry. I'll see nobody gets into trouble. Just leave it to me. You know, I'm sure there must be some reasonable explanation." His eyes brightened. "And who knows? There might even be a reward."

She smiled at him, loving him for the optimism that came bouncing back like a great red ball. She knew, however, there were things that could not be explained away, things she had not told him. Someone at Mallerton had lied. Someone at

187

Mallerton had planned to pass a copy off as an original. And there was only one person it could be: Sir Robert.

"Well, I've learned a lesson," her father was saying rather sadly. "I'm not in this class. Perhaps I'd better settle for being a copyist after all. Emily, I'm going to turn over a new leaf —"

"No, don't, Dad!" she said. "I like the old one. You go on painting. I don't care if the bailiffs come. I like candlelight! I even like cold tomato soup! Who wants to be rich?"

He looked at her, and she thought his eyes were wet.

"What's the matter?" she asked anxiously, but he smiled and said, "Oh, Emily, you're my brave girl."

She wasn't really brave, she thought when he had left her. Not yet . . . Her mother had once told her she was going through a difficult phase. Perhaps I'm coming out of it now, she thought, stretching her arms out in the moonlight, almost as if they were wings. I wonder what I shall turn into next.

21

They walked through the gates of Mallerton House unchallenged. The ticket lodge was closed. The sun was shining, and she was filled with a nervous excitement that made her want to go leaping down the drive. Emily wanted the visit to be over. She wanted to be going back home.

"What did he say?" she asked.

Her father had rung Sir Robert from the hotel, demanding to see him about an urgent matter, one he preferred not to discuss on the telephone.

"I told you."

"Tell me again. Every word."

"Let me see . . . 'Dodd,' he said, 'what's all this? Where are you ringing from? Swanham Bay? What the devil are you doing down here? No, I can't see you. I'm going up to London this morning.'"

"And what did you say?"

"I said, 'I think you'd better see me first, Sir Robert.' And Emily, he was *frightened!* He blustered and shouted, but I could tell. You know, I think he imagines I'm going to blackmail him. And all the time, I come bearing gifts!" He looked down at the kitbag in his hands and his face flushed with anger. "Damn him, he doesn't deserve it! Do you realize, *I* would have been involved. Who'd have believed I knew nothing about it? I might even have gone to prison! The man's a — a —" He seemed lost for a word low enough.

"Stinker?" suggested Emily, leaping a pothole with such exuberance that she only recovered her balance by a wild windmill of arms.

"Careful!" said her father. He looked at the neglected drive, the unkempt shrubs, and the tall trees strangled with ivy. "I suppose he was desperate. If you ask me, it'll take more than one Renoir to put this to rights. He'll have to sell. Can't live in the past forever, poor devil."

"Serve him right!" said Emily. "He's a beast."

"Not a likable man," her father agreed. "Stupid, too. Doesn't know a thing about art. How could he have expected to get away with it?"

190

"Dad, what would you have done if he'd asked you to fake it?"

"I'd have told him . . ." her father began, and then stopped. A thoughtful look came into his face. "A fifty-fifty split of whatever it fetched? You know, that's a great deal of money! And I could've made a proper job of it, if I'd known what he wanted. I know a trick or two . . ." Catching sight of her face, he smiled and admitted honestly, "I'd certainly have been tempted. Emily, we'd have been rich!"

"Yes," she said. For a moment her head filled with wistful dreams of all the things they could have done; then she smiled. "Oh well, I've got twenty pounds in the bank, if you're short."

They turned the last corner of the drive and saw, against the backdrop of the old, tired house, two boys standing side by side in the sunlight. Kevin and Oliver. Two pairs of eyes, one dark, one light, turned to stare at them, and then at the kitbag in Mr. Dodd's hands.

"You told, damn you!" Oliver screamed at her. "You broke your hand of honor!"

"Steady now," said her father. "Emily's told me nothing. It's you who've given the show away, jumping to conclusions like that. You must be Sir Robert's son. So it was you who hid the Renoir, was it?"

"Go away!" said Oliver hysterically. "Why do you have to interfere? You'll ruin everything! Take him away!" He turned on Emily. "Tell him it's all right!"

"I took the wrong painting," she confessed bravely.

The boys stared at her. Then Kevin laughed.

"Oh, Titch," he said, "if that ben't just like you."

He stopped laughing abruptly. Oliver had snatched the kitbag out of Mr. Dodd's hands and was off, away from the house and into the shrubs before the others had time to move.

"Come back!" cried Mr. Dodd, and began to run. Kevin and Emily soon outdistanced him. She glanced back over her shoulder and saw her father had slowed to a walk, puffing and holding his side. She ran on.

Oliver, for all his boasted ill health, was fast. She was just in time to see him vault the gate to the Maze and disappear. Next Kevin leapt over the gate, yards in front of Emily.

"Wait for me!" she panted, but of course he did

not wait, but vanished into the hedges like a brown bird.

Emily's legs felt like wet clay. As she opened the gate, she could hear the boys' voices. She hesitated. She knew the Maze by now and distrusted it. It seemed to have the habit of expanding and contracting at will, like a flesh-eating plant. She did not want to be hidden in leaves, like Sylvia. I like things to be open now, she thought. None of this would have happened if we hadn't all tried to hide from each other . . .

"Where are you?" she shouted.

There was silence. They weren't going to answer. They did not want her, the gawk, the outsider. Angrily, for she had thought them her friends, she walked through the gate, and the shadows of the tall hedges enclosed her. Now she could hear whispers. They seemed to be coming from every side, breathing through the dark, dusty leaves.

"Why do you always have to interfere?" said one. "I'm sick of you!"

"And I've had a bellyful of you!" said another.

"I don't care!" she shouted. "Go ahead and vomit!"

Silence.

She turned a corner, and suddenly she was there, in the heart of the Maze. It was a gray heart; even the sun could not do much with it — a grubby square of cracked concrete, with a rusty iron bench in the middle, a large plastic trash barrel on either side, and the two boys.

"We wasn't talking to you, Titch," said Kevin, his teeth white in his brown face. "We was just having a quarrel."

"A *private* quarrel," said Oliver. He was sitting on the bench, his face flushed and sullen. At his feet was the nylon kitbag, crumpled and obviously empty.

"What have you done with Sylvia?" Emily asked sharply.

"Put her where she belongs," he muttered.

She glanced at Kevin, who jerked his thumb toward one of the trash barrels. There was a roll of canvas sticking out of the top. She picked it up and unrolled it carefully, to see if it was damaged.

"Emily! Emily!" her father called in the distance. She did not answer. She was gazing down at the canvas. Sylvia looked back at her. The sun, shining through the leaves, dappled the pale face with restless shadows, and the painted eyes seemed to move as if looking for something, demanding something. No, thought Emily uneasily, letting the canvas roll up again. Go away! You're not real!

She looked at Oliver. "I didn't tell on you, honest," she said. "Dad found it. We've got to give it back. I'm sorry."

He shrugged. Then he bent down and, picking up the empty kitbag, threw it at Emily.

"All right, take it! Take it! I don't care! Do what you like with it! You've ruined my life, that's all."

"Ollie —" began Kevin, but Oliver turned on him fiercely.

"And you shut up! I've had more than enough of you! Look at him!" he said, turning to Emily. "Look at Kevin, the hero! Do you know what he wanted to do? He wanted to go to my father and tell him everything. Tell him he knew all about the fake, only of course he wasn't going to give me away! Oh no, not Kevin. He was going to pretend he'd taken it."

"Why?" asked Emily in amazement.

"*I* don't know! Something about my father going on . . . He just can't leave things alone. It was just the same when we were kids. 'Don't blame Oliver,' he'd say, before I had a chance to open my mouth, 'it was me.' He makes me sick."

"I was only trying to help," said Kevin. "I'm older than you."

"You're not older than my father! Why should you care what he does? What's it to you if he's caught? *You're* not his son! You're only a gypsy's brat!" He burst into tears. "I wish I were dead," he said.

Emily looked away, embarrassed for him. She caught Kevin's eye. He did not look hurt or angered by Oliver's attack, but simply fed up. Don't give him up now, she wanted to say, he didn't mean any of it. He needs you.

But Kevin turned away.

"Best wipe your nose," he said to Oliver, his voice hard. "You look a right mess. So you don't care if your dad goes to prison, then?"

"He doesn't care about me," Oliver mumbled. "He always liked you best."

"That's silly."

"He did! He did! You always had to be so brave! Always the one to stand up and take the blame! It's not fair! You never gave me a chance!"

Kevin flushed and was silent.

"Well, you've got a chance now, Oliver," said Emily. "Go on, it's your blame, take it! Tell your father. He can't do much, not after what *he's* done."

Oliver looked at her. His lips were trembling, and he put his hand up to hide them. "I — I can't!" he mumbled through his fingers, and hung his head.

She was sorry for him. She knew what it was like to be frightened and wanted to help him, but she did not know what to do. She glanced at Kevin, but he shrugged, his face sulky.

In the distance, a dog howled faintly. Or was it a cat? A thin, sad sound like a lost child calling . . .

Emily stopped dead. She lifted her head, listening. Then she looked back over her shoulder at Oliver.

"I dare you," she said, in a high, imperious voice, quite unlike her own. "I dare you. You have to do what I say, or I'll come and get you in the night."

He got up abruptly and stood staring at her, his eyes wide and blank. He took a step toward her, and she waited, holding her breath. But then he stopped and shook his head violently.

"You're not Sylvia!" he cried angrily. "You're

197

nothing like her! Anyway, I'm not mad. I know she's only a painting."

"Yes," she agreed, "she's only a painting. Still, it would've been a splendid end to the game, wouldn't it? Throw a double six and you're home. Oh well!" She turned toward the path and heard his voice behind her.

"You're going the wrong way," he said. "I suppose I'll have to show you. Show you both," he added, smiling uncertainly at Kevin.

Her father was waiting for them at the gate of the Maze. He saw the kitbag in Emily's hands and asked anxiously, "Is it all right?" She nodded.

"I'm sorry if I was rude," said Oliver stiffly. "Perhaps you would be good enough to wait in the library. I have something I must say to my father first."

"Good lad," said Mr. Dodd.

Oliver did not answer. He walked away with his head in the air. If his pace became slower as they entered the house, at least he did not stop. They walked down the long, shabby corridors in silence. His steps were now very slow indeed.

"Like me to come in with you?" asked Mr. Dodd.

"No, thank you."

He opened a door and showed them into a large, dim room, with books from ceiling to floor and stiff leather armchairs. It looked tidy and cold and unused.

"If you wouldn't mind waiting here," he said, very formally, looking at them with terrified eyes. Then he went, leaving the door open as if to show he was not going to run away. He crossed to the study door, knocked, and went in, closing the door behind him.

22

His father was standing by the window. He looked red and angry, as if something had happened already to upset him on this bright morning. Perhaps it was the sun he resented for showing up the flaws in Mallerton House.

"Oh, it's you," he said. "What is it, Oliver?"

Oliver's mouth was dry. His body was always a traitor. It was difficult to be brave when one's legs shook, one's heart seemed to have come loose in one's chest, and one's tongue felt like a stone.

The study was heavy with past humiliations. There was the desk before which he had stood trembling so often, while his father had bawled him out for a bad school report, or for failing to jump his horse over an easy fence, or for some ill-bred prank he and Kevin had committed. There was the chair over which he had bent to take his punishment, biting his lip to try and stop himself from crying out, but always, always ending in tears, the wretched tears that came unasked and unwanted, the tears his father despised him for.

Sometimes he had felt he almost hated Kevin for his dry eyes. For Kevin was whipped, too. Sir Robert was a great believer in corporal punishment. "Boys are like dogs and need to be shown who is master," he'd said. He blamed all the ills of modern society on the new softness of authority, and would like to have seen flogging brought back, yes, and hanging too. "Never did me any harm," he'd claim. "Short and sharp justice — better than a mouthful of sermons, what? Eh, boy?"

Oliver wished Kevin were here now. He did not really hate him, of course. Kevin was his friend, his best friend, who'd tried to give him courage, even though it was a gift Oliver found difficult to accept, fumbling it with his butterfingers as if it were a dropped catch.

"What is it?" his father said impatiently. "Come on, boy, don't stand there like a dummy. If you've something to say, say it. What is it you want? I hope it's not going to take too long. I haven't much time for you now. I'm expecting someone."

You never have much time for me, thought Oliver, and felt the shameful tears well up in his eyes.

"What the devil's the matter with you now? For heaven's sake, pull yourself together, boy!" his father said. "If you're not well, go to your mother, she'll know what to do. Give you some medicine — God knows she has enough bottles of the stuff in her bathroom. Or ask Mardie. I can't think why you're always ill." He made it sound like a crime.

"I can't help it!" burst out Oliver. "I don't do it on purpose!"

"No. Not your fault, I suppose. Take after your mother," said his father, making a visible effort to be kinder. Gentleness was not part of his nature and he wore it uneasily, like a bull decked out in daisy chains. "I don't mean to be hard on you, my boy. It's for your own good. After all, Mallerton will be yours one day, and you need to toughen up if you're going to be able to hold on to it. That doctor's a fool. It's fresh air and hard exercise you need, in my opinion, not all this lying in bed half the day. Too many women fussing over you. Made you soft. Come riding with me before breakfast every morning — that'll give you a healthy appetite, eh? Would you like that, Oliver?"

Oliver did not answer.

His father looked at him for a moment, then said, the impatience back in his voice, "Well, never mind. Run back to your mother now. I'm busy. Go on," he added as Oliver did not move, "away with you, boy!"

"*No!*"

The word rang out, full of defiance, carrying a courage that no one who was naturally brave and careless could possibly understand. Oliver, with the tears still wet on his cheeks, stood resolutely in front of the door, refusing to run back to his mother or his bed, refusing even to faint. The pity was, his father did not notice. He was looking moodily out of the window again and seemed to have forgotten Oliver was in the room. It was all to do again.

Yet Oliver felt almost happy. For the first time, he had refused a chance to escape from the hated study. "No" might be only a small word, but Oliver held on to it like a talisman. The other words would come; it was only the first that was so difficult. He knew he could do it now.

The clock ticked patiently on the mantelpiece, not hurrying him. It was strangely peaceful in this oasis of time. Someone walked heavily across the room above, and a small flake of plaster drifted down from the ceiling to land on his father's head. It lay grayish white on the chestnut hair, like an intimation of age. He'll grow old and feeble one day, thought Oliver, and I will be the man. I'll be kind to him, and wheel him about the grounds in his invalid chair. He'll look forward to my coming then; his dim eyes will brighten when he sees me. I'll take him down to the lake when the water lilies are in flower — and I'll push him in! He smiled at himself, knowing he would not really do it, or even want to; it comforted him to know it would be in his power to be kind. One day he would be strong. One day.

"Father," he said, his voice high and clear, "it was me who burned down the gallery. I did it."

In the library, Emily sat, straining her ears. There was silence at first, then she heard Sir Robert shouting. The furious sound seemed to shake the old house, making it creak and rattle.

"I'm going in there," said Kevin, but Mr. Dodd

put out a restraining hand. "Best for the boy if he can manage it himself," he said. Kevin flushed, and sat down again.

It seemed an endless wait. Then the door opened and Oliver stood there. He was pale and tear-stained, but he smiled with great determination.

"Father says you can come in now," he said.

23

Sir Robert was standing behind his desk, stiff as a poker and red as the fire. His hot, angry brown eyes examined them each in turn, stopping when they came to Kevin with a look of outrage.

"Who's this?" he demanded. "How many more of them are there? Is this another of yours, Dodd?"

"It's me, sir. Kevin. Kevin Dewy."

"Good God, boy, I didn't recognize you! You need a haircut. And what the devil's that thing in your ear? You look like a girl."

"No, I don't, sir, begging your pardon," said Kevin, unabashed. "It's how we look out there nowadays. It's the fashion, see? Though some of them shave their heads," he added fairly.

"I thought better of you. What are you doing here? We don't need you."

"He knows, Father," said Oliver.

"He knows, does he? I suppose I have you to thank for that! How many other people have you told?" said his father, turning on him irritably. "The groom? The kitchen maid?"

Now his eyes were on Emily; she met them as bravely as she could.

"There's no need to shout at my daughter," her father said, before Sir Robert had a chance to speak. "She's done you a good turn. She's a brave girl. You ought to thank her."

He didn't, of course. He merely said, "Brave, is she? She ran away fast enough yesterday. Should stop and face the music, you know. Well, what have you got to say for yourself?"

"Would you really have shot me?"

He stared, gave a snort, possibly intended as a laugh, and said, "Shoot the whole lot of you, if I got the chance." He turned to Mr. Dodd: "I understand from my son you have something of mine."

Mr. Dodd took the canvas gently out of the bag and handed it over.

"Careful!" he said, as the baronet unrolled it roughly.

"It's been torn at the corner," Sir Robert said accusingly.

"Good grief, man! You're lucky to have it back at all," said Mr. Dodd angrily. "Luckier than you deserve. I want an explanation, sir."

Sir Robert put the painting down on the desk slowly, moving an ashtray to make room for it, letting them all wait. He had not asked them to sit down and obviously had no intention of doing so.

"There seems to be a misunderstanding," he said coldly. "My son told me some cock-and-bull story. Can't make head or tail of it. I employed you, Dodd, to make a copy of this painting, as I intended to sell it and wanted something to hang in its place. You did your work reasonably well, and I paid you for it. I can't see what more there is to be said."

"Father . . ." began Oliver.

"You be quiet, boy!"

Emily looked at her father, who seemed to be having some difficulty choosing his words. She waited hopefully for the explosion, but it did not come. Mr. Dodd caught sight of Oliver, standing pale and upright by his father's side, and when he spoke, it was quite mildly.

"Well, that's one way of putting it, I suppose," he said. "By the way, I'd like to see my copy again before I go."

There was a definite suggestion in his voice that if his request was not granted, there would be trouble. The two men stood looking at one another, while the children watched them and held their breath. Then Sir Robert said, not giving an inch, "It's not your property anymore, Dodd. If you want to see it, come back in the summer and buy a ticket at the gate, like any other tourist."

"And will it be there?" said Mr. Dodd.

"What do you mean by that, sir? I'm telling you, Dodd, if I hear you've been slandering me, I shall sue!"

"And welcome!" said Mr. Dodd, losing his temper. "I'm not bloody leaving here till I've seen it!"

"Father!" said Oliver. His voice was loud, almost sharp, and he met his father's eyes unflinchingly.

His father hesitated; then, abruptly opening a drawer, he took out a roll of canvas and threw it down on the desk.

Mr. Dodd picked it up and carried it over to the table by the window, where he spread it out, holding it down with his hands.

"Dear me, it seems to have aged considerably since I last saw it," he said.

"Some fool of a servant leaned it against a radiator. Cracked the paint."

Mr. Dodd raised his eyebrows.

"A very hot radiator. I suppose the stretcher warped and that's why it's been removed?" he suggested obligingly.

"Yes."

"An extremely hot radiator. Curious, I can't seem to see my name on it. A copy by Benjamin Dodd. Perhaps that flaked off too? Quite a history of accidents."

Sir Robert's complexion darkened from red to purple, but he stood unblinking, stiff as a soldier on parade.

"I'll see it's on again, Dodd. I suppose you want your credit, like anybody else. You can leave it to me."

There was a long pause. Then Mr. Dodd said slowly, "Yes. Yes, I think I can now." He let the canvas roll up again and left it on the table. "Good thing you're an honest man," he said, "or you might have tried to pass this off as an original. And landed up in prison. Good Lord, the youngest lad at Sotheby's, with eggshell still on him, wouldn't have been taken in for a moment! Not one moment!"

Sir Robert was silent.

"Come on, Emily," said her father. "Kevin?"

"I'm coming," he said.

Emily did not want to go. She thought Sir Robert was getting off too lightly. She wanted to tell him exactly what she thought of him, and had got as far as opening her mouth when she caught sight of Oliver's face. She turned and followed her father.

They were nearly at the door when Sir Robert called out, "Kevin!"

They all turned.

"If you want a job when you leave school . . ." he said. "You'd have to cut your hair, though. Can't have one of my staff looking like a damned gypsy."

Emily looked at Kevin. To her disgust, he answered politely. "Why, thank you, sir. But I don't want no job. Going to travel. Right round the world — India, China, Africa . . ." His dark eyes shone. "I'll see 'em all! Got money saved as will take me to France already," he said proudly.

"And I can work — but not in one place. Got itchy feet — suppose it's the gyppo in me. Still, thank you, sir."

Sir Robert took out his wallet, extracted a note, and held it out. "Come on, boy, take it," he said impatiently. "Get a haircut!"

It was a ten-pound note.

All eyes fastened on it. Then they looked at Kevin. He knew what Emily wanted. She wanted him to tear up the note and throw it in Sir Robert's face. But he could not do it. He was never a boy to hit someone when he was down. Besides, ten pounds was ten pounds! He took the note, folded it up carefully, and put it in the pocket of his jeans.

"Thank you, sir," he said, smiling up into the heavy red face, sensing dimly the cold shame behind the fierce eyes. He added cheekily, "But I won't be using it for no haircut."

Sir Robert laughed.

"Get out!" he said roughly. "Be off with you, you young devil, before I take it back."

They walked away from the house.

"How could you take it?" asked Emily. "It was a bribe, a bribe to keep you quiet!"

"Money's money," said Kevin. "Ten pounds! Take me another hundred miles or thereabouts! Besides, I dunno. Poor old beggar!"

"The man's an idiot," said Mr. Dodd. "Those cracks! Scratched on with a pin and dirt rubbed into them — you could see it with the naked eye. I don't envy his son. The man's a —" He swallowed what he was going to say, obviously thinking it unfit for their ears.

"Fooled us, didn't he, though?" said Kevin. "He ben't really like that. Acting it up a bit. And not a one of us as dared tell him to his face he was a cheat! He's not one to apologize, is Sir Robert." He sounded as if he admired him for it. Seeing Emily's face, he explained, "Got courage. Not much else, though."

He turned and looked back at the house. It lay in its grounds, warm in the sunshine, looking half asleep.

"He loves Mallerton. Can't last much longer." He sounded sad, as if he had loved it a little, too. "Suppose they'll pull it down."

"Good thing," said Emily.

"Thought you wanted a big house, Titch."

"Not any longer, thank you! Perhaps I'll come with you on your travels . . ."

"Wait till you're asked. Ben't sure I want no girls hanging on, getting blisters, muddling things up. You get back in your frame, Sylvia!"

"I'm Emily!" she shouted, and chased him down the long drive, laughing, glad to be away from the sad house, not wanting to think of Oliver and his father anymore.

Only when they reached the gates and stopped to wait for her father did she say anxiously, "What will happen to Oliver? Will he be all right?"

"Don't see why not."

"Will you go on seeing each other?"

He shrugged, frowning.

"Dunno. Ben't easy," he said. "Cheer up, Titch. He'll be all right now. He'll have friends of his own sort."

Her father caught up with them and they said no more. Mr. Dodd asked Kevin why he wasn't at school. Kevin coughed unconvincingly, decided against pretending to be ill, and said cheerfully, "First offense. Never done it afore. They won't make much fuss — I got a good reputation."

Mr. Dodd smiled.

"Lucky boy," he said. He then asked Kevin to come and stay with them during the holidays. Lots of good street markets in London. They could buy things and polish them up — make a fortune!

"Don't mind if I do," said Kevin, looking pleased.

"Only no faking," said Emily sternly.

"No, no!" they said, looking innocent.

They were already on the bus, waiting for it to start, when they heard the sound of a horse, galloping fast, and saw through the windows Oliver riding out of the gates and along the grass shoulder, reining in his horse with a great flurry of hooves.

"I did it! I did it! I did it!" he shouted triumphantly, his face alight with excitement. "Kev, I did it!"

"Yeah! Well done, Ollie! You was splendid!" called Kevin, laughing and waving as the bus started up.

"Come and see me! We'll go riding together! Bring Emily!" Oliver was riding along the grass, keeping pace with the slowly moving bus.

"Yeah! Thanks! I'd like that!" shouted Kevin.

The bus put on speed.

"We'll be friends, all three of us, forever!" they heard Oliver shout as the bus drew away from him. They sat, craning their necks, seeing the boy on the horse rein up and wave. Then he was out of sight.

Emily sat back in her seat. She remembered Kevin's mother had said, "They'll grow apart — they won't mean to, but they will. It's the way of the world."

"We'll change the world," she said.

Her father looked at her in surprise.

"That's a big ambition," he said, smiling. Then he thought for a moment, and said quietly, "I wish you luck."